Rennillia:Prequel

Rennillia Series
M. Sembera

Rennillia:Prequel

Rennillia Series
By M. Sembera

ISBN-13: 978-0692654859
ISBN-10: 0692654852

Sometimes, you have to go back to the beginning
to get to the end.

Table of Contents

I'm not a fan of reliving the past, especially mine. This isn't exactly the beginning but it is the start of everything. Back before I knew the truth, back when we were far from innocent but completely naive. I was 15 and rebellious. My only friend was Hert and all I wanted, was to get out of my parent's house. This is the story of our friendship, meeting Emerson, dating Jackson, losing myself and what I now believe to be the starting point of our future. -Ren

I laid across my bed, relieved the house was finally quiet, after listening to my father yell for four straight hours. He was in one of his moods. Who was I kidding, all he ever did was yell. Nothing ever went right for him and nothing was ever good enough for that man. Truthfully, around the hundredth time I heard him tell my mother she ruined his life, I was happy he was so miserable. She wasn't any better. At least he yelled. My mother hardly said a word. No 'I love you' or 'How was your day', just the occasional 'Do what your father tells you.' Maybe, I had ruined both their lives. But with my sixteenth birthday two weeks away and the idea of having only two years of juvenile hell left as a minor, I thought about how wonderful eighteen would be. I would be out of their house and on my own.

Chapter 1

I turned my lamp off and curled up in my comforter. As I drifted off, I heard a knock at my window. Startled at first, I was relieved to see it was Hert standing outside. I turned my lamp on before walking over to open my window. When I did, he stepped back and motioned for me to come outside.

Climbing out of my window, I whispered, "What are you doing here?"

Shaking his head, Hert informed, "I came to tell you bye."

"Where are you going?"

"My mother can put up with him all she wants but…" he started before I stopped him, suggesting, "Okay, come inside before the neighbors see you."

Hesitant at first, he followed me through the window and into my room.

"Is your father still awake?"

Shaking my head, I looked up at him and gasp, "What happened?"

I hadn't notice outside in the dark, he was beat up.

"What do you think?"

"Are you okay?" I asked as I walked into the bathroom and grabbed a towel.

Scowling at me, he nodded.

"Stay here, I'm gonna get you some ice."

"I don't need it. I came to tell you I was leaving," he stated as he smoothed his messy black hair away from his forehead.

Starting to get upset, I fussed, "You can't leave."

"Well, I am," Hert snapped and turned toward the window.

Thinking quickly, I offered, "Stay with me."

Turning back toward me, he shook his head, saying, "Your father's never gonna let me stay here."

With a smile, I shared, "Then we won't tell him."

Hert started to argue with me as I persuaded, "They never come in here and their rooms are all the way on the other side of the house."

Giving me an unsure expression, he replied, "That's a really bad idea."

"I know, but it'll just be for a little while until we figure something out. Besides I'll never forgive you for leaving me, I'll be mad at you forever."

Narrowing his eyes at me, Hert conceded and sat down on a little bench seat next to my bed.

After quietly leaving the room, I quickly returned with ice for his eye. Hert didn't say anything about his father or anything else; he just sat there looking angry. Not long after the ice melted we went to sleep.

I slept for a few hours before opening my eyes to look at the clock. It was five thirty, which gave us little time to figure out how to get Hert out of the house before school started. Sitting up, I looked over at Hert. He had slept sitting up on my bench. His arms were folded tight against his chest. Wishing he would open his eyes, the clear blue always softened his appearance. Smiling slightly as I watched him, I thought he looked angry even in his sleep. No wonder I was his only friend. Most people were put off by Hert, but I liked him. He was quick to argue or get in a fight and most of the time he appeared unhappy. That is what I liked about him though, it made the rare times when he was happy or actually smiled memorable and special.

Picking up one of the smaller pillows off my bed, I threw it at him. Laughing a little when he immediately jumped to his feet, I watched him pick it up and throw it back at me.

Still laughing, I said, "Good Morning Sunshine," as I watched him walk to my bathroom.

Stretching out on my bed, I thought of a plan.

Although it wasn't unusual for Hert to show up at school with black eyes or bruises, I thought it might be a good idea for both of us to skip a day.

Hert walked out of the bathroom, asking, "Shouldn't you be getting ready?"

Shaking my head at him, I replied, "We aren't going today."

"Oh, we're not?"

Smiling wide, I shared, "My father's leaving for some job thing this morning. He won't be back for a few days and you know my mother couldn't care less what I do, so I'm sick."

Giving me a suspicious look, Hert said, "You don't look sick."

Frustrated, he wasn't excited about my plan, I snapped, "You afraid Carmella's gonna get mad?"

"What?" he snapped back, appearing surprised.

Shaking my head at him, I explained, "I know you see her."

"Don't be stupid, Renni."

"I'm not stupid, you are for…" I started before I heard my father's voice.

Quickly hopping off the bed, I warned, "Stay here, I'll be right back."

Putting on my best sick face, I slowly walked into the kitchen.

My mother was standing in front of the stove cooking breakfast while my father sat at the table. Slowly pulling out one of the chairs, I slunk down in it and laid my head down on the table.

"What's wrong with you?" my father grumbled.

Looking over at him, I pouted, "I don't feel good."

"Why not?"

Shrugging my shoulders, I answered, "I just feel sick."

Ignoring my pretend sickness, my father questioned, "Do you know what that boy did?"

I could have asked what boy, but why pretend. I knew he was talking about Hert. I just shook my head at him.

"That disrespectful teppista got himself into a fight with Charles then ran off," he shared with an 'I told you so' tone.

Even though he was sitting in my room, I asked, "Do they know where he is?"

Still condescending in tone my father assured, "That mother of his is looking for him."

It was hard for me to keep pretending to be sick when my father was bad mouthing Hert.

Really, I couldn't see how Hert was wrong? How dare he try to stop his father, Charles, from hitting his mother? As bad as my own father was, I never saw him raise a hand to my mother. I was another story altogether. It was different with me of course. First, I was his kid and second, I imagine if I silently obeyed my father like my mother did it would be different. I guess I kind of knew my behavior was disrespectful at times but there was only so much respect I was willing to pay someone who wished I wasn't here at all. Except recently, my father seemed pleased to have me as a daughter. All he talked about was some stupid dinner I was ordered to attend with him at the Roberts's house on Friday.

Putting my need to defend my friend to the side, I realized, I had a great idea.

"I'm really worried," I pouted, still trying to sound sick.

Angry, my father yelled, "You don't need to worry about that boy!"

Shaking my head at him, I whined, "Not about that. I'm feeling really sick, what if I'm not better by Friday?"

My father's tone changed instantly as he ordered, "I'll be home Friday morning; I don't want you going to school until I get back."

Nodding, I asked, "Can I just eat in my room then?"

"Fix your plate then go back to bed," he stated as he waited for my mother to serve him.

Making it way more dramatic than necessary, I filled a plate with eggs, sausage and biscuits before slowly shuffling back to my room.

Closing my door and locking it behind myself, I smiled wide.

"We're good. I don't have to go to school until Friday."

Hert took the plate as I handed it to him, asking, "Is this for me?"

Nodding, I grabbed a biscuit and sat down next to him.

In between bites, Hert asked, "So how did you pull that off?"

"Cause, I'm a genius."

Rolling his eyes at me, Hert finished his breakfast.

When he was done, I took the plate and set it on my dresser.

"Do you wanna take a shower?" I asked, noticing he was pretty dirty.

Shrugging, he said, "Yea, but..." before I interrupted him, saying, "I think I have some of your clothes in my drawer from the last time we were out at the pond. I'll throw your dirty clothes in the washer."

"Your mother won't wonder why you're washing my clothes?"

"No. Whenever he leaves she just stays in her room. I think she's depressed or something. I know I would be if I were married to that man."

Nodding, Hert stood up and walked to my bathroom.

After his shower, I handed him his clean clothes and took his dirty ones to the laundry room. When I got back to my room, Hert was stretched out across my bed asleep. Thinking, a little nap wouldn't hurt me either, I carefully laid down next to him.

I watched him sleeping for a while, thinking how much I would miss him if he really did leave. The majority of our time was spent arguing or being mad at each other but we were the same. Well, he was considerably more responsible than me but usually I could talk him into almost anything. On the one hand, it was exciting to be so close to freedom but on the other hand, I worried what would happen when we did grow up. Carmella wasn't his girlfriend but he did see her. Although he had said once it was just a thing, which meant they didn't go out, he just slept with her now and then. I wondered if that was true, and if it was, for how long? I had never even had an actual boyfriend and Hert was already sleeping with someone.

All boyfriend/girlfriend conversations were banned after I told Hert that when Jimmy Marcello kissed me he grabbed my butt and Hert beat him up at school the next day. After that, we agreed it was best not to share everything. Technically, I wasn't allowed to date. Something about how young ladies are supposed to behave and some other stupid thing my father made up about waiting for the right opportunity to make my life miserable. However, I didn't really care. I didn't want a boyfriend. It all seemed like too much trouble. The girls in class were always saying how their boyfriend's liked this or didn't like that and how they wanted them to dress. Hert was better than a boyfriend. I never had to pretend with him. The longer I spent dwelling on it, the more I realized I wasn't going to get any sleep.

I must have watched Hert sleep for about an hour before he opened his eyes.

"Were you watching me sleep?" he mumbled as he sat up.

"Sorta, I was thinking."

Making a disturbed face at me, he said, "That's not creepy."

Shaking my head, I rolled my eyes, asking, "Why do you see Carmella?"

"Don't start Renni," he fussed before I snapped at him, "I was seriously asking. I mean what if you get her pregnant? Is she someone you'd want to marry?"

Making a face at me, he said, "She's not going to get pregnant."

"Oh, you know that for a fact?"

Appearing serious, Hert assured, "Yes, I do."

"I just don't understand, I mean..." before Hert cut me off, saying, "I know how you feel about sex because of your parents, but seriously you're not even curious? I mean are you really gonna go your whole life without it?"

Shrugging, I replied, "It just doesn't seem like it's worth ruining lives. What's wrong with just not? I would rather grow up and be friends with you than be married and have kids."

"I'm never getting married but that's different."

"How is it different?"

With a shrug Hert said, "It's hard to explain."

Feeling inspired, I sat up and announced, "You and I should live together after graduation."

"What? Where did that come from?"

Smiling wide, I said, "Just think, it would be perfect. If neither of us are getting married then why not. I'll cook for you and listen to you complain and you'll work and let me smack you around every now and then, you know, so it feels like home."

"Oh you're real funny," he laughed as he tackled me.
Rolling around on my bed, he held my arms as I tried to break free. Laughing too, I stopped struggling for a moment. There was a time when we were more evenly matched but now that we were older it was easy for him to out muscle me.

"Now what are you gonna do?" he laughed.
With a wicked smile, I leaned up and licked him right across his face. Immediately letting go, he jumped off the bed wiping his face off with his arm.

"That's just sick Renni," he fussed as I rolled onto my stomach and laughed into my pillow.

More at a giggle now, I patronized, "Aww, did I upset you."

"Now I know why you've never had a boyfriend," he smirked.

His comment stung a little so I snapped, "I'm just a little more selective then some people."
I was pleased my comment made him mad.

We didn't say a word to each other for the rest of the day. As it got to be later in the evening, I made us sandwiches. After throwing a blanket on the floor for Hert to lie on, I went to sleep thinking of different ways to irritate him the next day.

Chapter 2

Quickly sitting up, I glanced at Hert who was on his feet when there was a knock on my bedroom door. I motioned for him to go into the bathroom while I unlocked my door and stepped into the hallway.

"Have you heard from Scott?" My mother asked.

As I shook my head, she informed, "Abigail called, Charles moved out. If you do hear from him tell him he needs to go home."

"Yes ma'am," I agreed before she said, "I have to go, I will be back this evening."

Nodding at her, I turned and shut my door, locking it behind myself.

Swinging the bathroom door open, I said, "Your father moved out. Your mother told mine."

The look on his face was stunned yet relieved. I was so happy for him I almost hugged him.

We stood in the bathroom quietly staring at each other for a while before Hert said, "I guess I'd better get home then."

"Now?"

He appeared confused, saying, "I wasn't going to stay here forever."

Nodding, I offered, "My mother's leaving, at least let me make us breakfast before you go."

Nodding, Hert agreed.

With my mother gone for the day, Hert and I went to the kitchen. After I made breakfast, we sat at the table eating. I was sad to see him going home but happy it would be peaceful from now on. When breakfast was over Hert helped me clean up the kitchen. As we washed the dishes I started flicking water at him. Several serious glances later, he started playing back and both of us were laughing until the back door slammed shut. Hert stepped half way in front of me. All I could do was watch my father's face turning red as I stared wide eyed at him.

"Boy, you better get outta my house!" My father shouted.

I started defending Hert and I, saying, "We weren't doing anything."

Before my father could respond, Hert stated, "Sir, it's my fault."

My father's voice boomed as he hollered, "How dare you speak to me you worthless bastard, find some other little whore to…"

I stopped my father's rant, shouting, "It was my fault."

Hert looked down at me, saying, "Renni."

Looking up at him, I pleaded, "Go home, please."

Hert walked to the front door after assuring, "Mr. Cantinelli, I apologize for being here without your permission. I would never disrespect your daughter."

When the door shut, I braced myself. Familiar with what was about to occur, I could have begged and pleaded, swore that nothing happened but it wouldn't have made a difference. I would just prolong the inevitable. It was one of those situations where your first instinct is to run but I covered my face with my arms instead.

As my father tried to beat some obedience into me, I thought about Hert getting to go back home. At the end, he pulled my arms away from my face.

"I better not catch that boy anywhere near this house again," he shouted before grabbing my face with his hand and yelling, "That's all I need, for you to get knocked up."

As he let go, I stated, "Yes, sir," and walked to my room.

Lying on my bed, I started wondering how long it would be before I had to hear yelling again. I got my answer when my door flew open and my father stormed in.

Throwing a box at me, he yelled, "You're staying home the rest of the week."

"Yes, sir," I spouted.

"And you're wearing a dress on Friday," he informed before slamming my door.

Kicking the dress box off my bed, I curled up into my comforter.

Later in the evening, I heard my father hollering and knew my mother had returned. I couldn't tell what he was saying; I only noticed his voice getting closer to my door.

"What did I do now?" I shouted as he yanked me out of bed and drug me into the kitchen.

"A man can't trust the women in his own house! This is why I came back early! Now where was she?" he shouted, jerking me around to face my mother.

"Sir?"

"Ya'll are both the same! Both of you! Mignotta, merdoso!"

I was instantly offended. Not that he said I was a filthy whore but that he compared me to my mother. I had done just about everything in my power, talk out of turn, break the rules as often as possible, in order to not be silently obedient like her.

Before I could help it, I shouted back at him, "I am nothing like her!"

The look of hurt on my mother's face wasn't as surprising as the back of my father's hand across my mouth. He had never hit me in the face before. My eyes instantly welled up with tears which upset me even more.

From about the age of thirteen, I refused to cry. If I cried, it was like I was saying I was sorry. I was never sorry. I took my licks, so to speak, with a sense of pride. I took great pride in the knowledge that my father could not control me.

I reached up touching my lip, looking at my bloody fingers I heard my father shout, "Look what you made me do!" to my mother before storming off to his room and slamming the door behind himself.

I knew why my father was upset and it had nothing to do with hurting me. He had busted my lip, which meant, I would have a big fat lip when we went to dinner at the Roberts' house. I glanced at my mother. She looked right past me and walked to her room. Grabbing a paper towel, I opened the freezer and placed a hand full of ice in it. I walked to my room and then to my bathroom to survey the damage. It wasn't that bad. After washing my mouth out, I laid across my bed holding ice to my lip. Once it stopped bleeding, I checked it again, finding it slightly swollen with only one small slit on my bottom lip. I have to admit, I was disappointed. My mouth hurt like hell and was throbbing but it would hardly be noticeable for the dinner.

Crawling back into bed, I wrapped the comforter all the way around myself. After trying hard to fall asleep, I gave up when I realized it wasn't going to happen. I unwrapped the comforter from around myself, reached down and grabbed the dress box off of the floor. I opened the box and found a little gray dress. It was pretty. However, I was still resentful enough not to try it on. I placed it back in the box and threw the box back on the floor. Flinging myself back to a lying position, I glanced over and saw Hert's wallet sitting on the bench by my bed. Smiling to myself, I thought, 'what kind of person would I be, if I didn't return it as soon as possible'. Hopping up off my bed, I pulled on a pair of jeans, sticking his wallet in my back pocket. Sliding my shoes on, I walked to my window and opened it.

Hert's house was four blocks from mine. If I cut through the back way, something we always did as kids, it only took about ten minutes to get there. Slowly creeping up to his window, I could see him perfectly. He was lying on his bed with his arms folded behind his head, staring at the ceiling. I tapped on his window and watched him get out of bed and walk toward me.

Smiling as he opened the window, I climbed in saying, "Whatcha' doin?"

Shaking his head, he asked, "You're not in enough trouble already?"

"I'm not worried about it," I assured, sitting down on his bed.

Hert narrowed his eyes at me asking, "What happened to your lip?"

Giving him a stupid look, I said, "What do you think."

Starting to pace back and forth, Hert clenched his fists saying, "I knew it was a bad idea."

I narrowed my eyes at him as I stated, "Just stop. First of all I knew what would happen if my father found out." I pointed to my mouth before continuing to say, "And second, this was not because of you."

In disbelief he snapped, "So he didn't do anything when I left?"

I laughed a little, saying, "Oh, I caught a beat down but he back handed me when I yelled at him after my mother got home."

Shaking his head at me, Hert sat down on his bed next to me.

We just stared at each other for a few minutes. I figured he was thinking of things to be mad at me about. While I kept thinking, I wish he would come back to my house.

Visibly irritated, he took a deep breath.

"You shouldn't have asked me to stay or I shouldn't have agreed. Why did you do that if you knew what was going to happen?"

Now, I was irritated.

Scowling at him, I snapped, "Really?"

Shaking his head, Hert offered, "I won't put you in that position again."

"You didn't put me in any position, ya jerk," I fussed as I started to get up.

Hert grabbed my shoulder, trying to stop me. He immediately let go when I winced.

"Let me see," he snapped.

Rubbing my fingertips across my forehead, I assured, "No, I'm fine."

I was fine, that is until I saw the look of anguish on his face.

His tone was soft as he asked, "Let me check and see if you're okay."

He looked so upset I couldn't say no.

Turning my back to him, I stared at the wall as he lifted the back of my shirt up.

When he gently placed his hand flat against my back, and breathed, "Renni," my eyes got a little watery.

Feeling embarrassed, I stood up.

"It's not that bad. It doesn't even hurt."

"Why do you do that?"

Quickly turning to face him, I snapped, "I'm not doing anything. And for your information, Hert, I don't need you looking at me all pitiful either. I'm a big girl now. I can take care of myself."

"Yea, I can tell."

"You're such an ass!"

"Because I don't want you to get hurt?"

"No, because you don't get it."

"What don't I get?"

Shaking my head at him, I explained, "You're my favorite person in the whole entire world, Hert. You're always worth the fight. That man doesn't get to wake up one day and decide I can't be friends with you anymore, and I'm never gonna let anyone come between us."

I waited for a minute for him to say something. When he only stared at me, I took his wallet out of my back pocket.

"You left this in my room."

I tossed the wallet on his bed, then climbed out his window and walked home.

Chapter 3

Friday started off busy. It was a little odd how happy my father was behaving. He almost appeared giddy. He took me into town, bought me a new pair of shoes to match the dress he gave me, and even took me to get my hair done. If I didn't know better, I would have thought he simply wanted to spend the day with me. However, knowing how he was, I understood. He wanted to make a good impression on the Roberts'.

I absolutely love dresses, but I really wasn't a fan of wearing them. As silly as that sounds, I usually only wore a dress once before it was banished to the back of my closet, forever. Not because I didn't like re-wearing clothes, I just preferred jeans and a t-shirt.

My hair was always unruly, and I could never quite get it to behave. My idea of fixing it consisted of pulling it up in a ponytail. I'm sure my father was afraid I would show up to the Roberts' house looking like a mess.

Carefully pulling my dress over my head, as not to mess up my hair, I stood in front of the mirror. It wasn't really my style of dress, I liked long sundresses that brushed the tops of my feet when I walked, but it was nice. It was light gray with cap sleeves and fell right above my knees.

Ready to go and get the dinner over with, I grabbed my new shoes, walked out of my room, and into the kitchen.

Taking one look at me, my father fussed, "You're not going to wear makeup?"

Turning to go back to my room, I mumbled, "I guess so," under my breath.

In my room, I leaned over the bathroom counter as I put my makeup on. When I did, I noticed several finger print bruises on the back of my arm. Sighing, I finished fixing my makeup, then walked to my closet. Trying again, I grabbed a little black cardigan out of my closet before heading back to the kitchen.

My father inspected me closely. I could tell he was looking at my bottom lip, checking to see if the mark he left on it was noticeable. It was much better and barely noticeable with lipstick, so unless someone was really staring, you couldn't tell.

As I started to put my sweater on, my father snapped, "Can't you ever just do what I want?"
With a sarcastic smile, I raised my arm and showed him why I was wearing it. He made no comment about the bruises. He just rushed me out the door and into the car.

On the way to the Roberts' house, my father went on and on about proper behavior and making a good impression. Just when I thought I would lose my mind if I heard him say 'young lady' again, we pulled up to the house.

My eyes almost popped out of my head, when I saw where the Roberts' lived. I had never seen anything like it. I'd seen two story houses before, Hert lived in one, but this place was massive. It was the size of at least three houses sitting on top of each other and five set side by side, from my neighborhood.

After my father parked the car, we walked a long pathway to the front door.
Before my father knocked, he informed, "This is the biggest opportunity of your life. Don't screw it up."
I begrudgingly nodded as he knocked. The door quickly opened and we were shown inside.

There was marble and crystal everywhere. The entire living room was bright, like a diamond catching the sunlight. As I glanced towards the stairs, I saw the most beautiful woman I had ever seen, in real life. Between her elegantly styled brown hair, and flawlessly tan skin, she was the picture of perfection from head to toe. As she made her way down the stairs, I watched a man follow behind her. Equally perfect with his broad shoulders and impeccable suit, I knew he was her other half.

My father took a step back as he placed his hand on my shoulder.

"Rennillia, this is Mr. and Mrs. Roberts."

I was too overwhelmed to speak. Smiling, I politely nodded at them.

Mrs. Roberts walked right up to me, saying, "Deangelo, she's absolutely lovely."

My father smiled with pride as Mr. Roberts escorted him into the other room.

"Have a seat, dear," Mrs. Roberts offered.

With another polite nod, I replied, "Yes, ma'am."

Taking the seat across from me, she stated, "Emerson will be down in just a moment. His basketball game ended late." Continuing to smile at me, she added, "You and he are the same age."

Nodding, I replied, "I'll be sixteen next week."

Seemingly excited, she asked, "Are you having a party, dear?"

"Oh, no, ma'am."

Appearing a bit disappointed, she offered, "We can have a dinner for you here."

Confused, I politely smiled.

Did I miss something? As nice as she seemed, I thought Mrs. Roberts might be a little on the crazy side. Here I was, a complete and total stranger, and she wants to have a birthday dinner for me. I looked around, suddenly feeling uncomfortable when the thought occurred to me that she might think I needed charity or something like that.

As I glanced up, I saw Emerson standing at the bottom of the stairs. I didn't know him, but I had seen him many times at school. He was already sixteen, although he could have easily passed for twenty. Emerson was one of those boys that were so handsome you could just stare at them for hours. Now that I had seen his parents, I knew where he got it from. He was a good foot taller than me, and did I mention how handsome he was? Most girls were dying to go out with him. In fact, his current girlfriend sat right in front of me in English class. All she ever talked about was his new car, his money, and all the fancy places he took her.

For me, knowing that Emerson belong to an elite upper-class of wealth and privilege caused me have the opposite feeling. Normally, I judged people by how they treated Hert. Even though I never saw them interact, I was sure someone like Emerson would look down on him. I will admit, if I had to be stuck at a dinner with my father and a deranged party throwing stranger, at least I had something pleasant to look at.

Emerson sat down on the other end of the couch. Feeling even more uncomfortable than before, I noticed Mrs. Roberts glancing back and forth between the two of us with a pleased expression on her face.

"I will be upstairs. Rennillia, it was a pleasure to meet you, dear," Mrs. Roberts announced as she stood up.

"Yes, ma'am, it was nice to meet you too."

Once she disappeared up the stairs, the room was quiet.

Emerson broke the silence, asking, "Do you play pool?"

Shrugging, I replied, "Not regularly."

Wearing an amused smile, he asked, "Would you like to play?"

I took a second to consider if I should say yes before I answered.

"Sure."

Emerson stood up and motioned for me to follow.

I followed him through the living room and into the kitchen. Before we made it to the back door, my father and Mr. Roberts walked around the corner. Mr. Roberts had a serious expression on his face, while my father's reflected a gratified disposition.

"Let's go," my father stated, taking notice of me standing next to Emerson.

Looking up at Emerson, I halfway apologized, "Maybe some other time."

Emerson glanced down at me, then looked directly at my father.

"If I bring her home later, can Rennillia stay?"

"Her curfew is midnight."

I looked to Mr. Roberts for approval as he offered, "You're welcome to stay."

With a slight smile, I nodded before we continued out of the back door.

Mentally questioning what the hell was going on, it was strange enough for Mrs. Roberts to offer to have me over for my birthday. Then, there was the dinner, where there was no dinner. Now, not only was my father letting me stay with Emerson, I had until midnight. Whatever Mr. Roberts and my father discussed must have made my father very happy, because I was never allowed to do anything.

Walking through a little covered area, we stepped into the garage. It was big enough to fit twenty cars and right to the left was a pool table.

"Would you like something to drink?" Emerson asked.

Shaking my head, I answered, "No, thank you."

Smiling at me, he handed me a stick and we started to play.

Although, I was horrible at it, I was having a lot of fun.

Not that I minded, but I had to ask, "Hey, why did you ask for me to stay?"

Questioning my question, he asked, "Were you ready to leave?"

Narrowing my eyes at him, I stated, "You didn't answer my question."

"I wanted to get to know you better."

Confused, I asked, "Don't you have a girlfriend?"

"We're playing pool not making out." Emerson replied with a slight laugh.

Embarrassed, I admitted, "I don't think that came out the way I meant it to." I continued to try and save face, by saying, "Your girlfriend is in one of my classes and she doesn't seem like the kinda girl that would be okay with this."

"Will your boyfriend care?"

"I don't have a boyfriend."

"Oh, I thought you were with that one guy, Scott. Y'all are always together."

Laughing at the thought, I blurted, "Hert?"

Emerson gave me a confused look.

"Long story, but Scott Herterand is Hert."

Nodding in confirmation, he pressed, "He's not your boyfriend? The two of you are always together."

"Our parents... Well, our fathers are friends. We grew up together. We're like family I guess, but better."

Emerson nodded, again, and we continued our game.

Not much time passed before I noticed him staring at me.

"Is there something you wanna say?" I questioned, raising my eyebrows at him.

As if he was trying hard to comprehend something, he asked, "Did you and he get into a fight?"

"Me and Hert?" When he nodded I snapped, "No, Why?"

"I'm not trying to make you mad, I only asked because both of you missed school, then he came back with a black eye, and you look like someone hit you in the lip."

I couldn't help smiling a little when I realized he must have been staring at my lips in order to notice. Incredibly flattered, I almost wished I had a thing for him.

"They're unrelated." I assured, quickly dispelling whatever thought he had.

Appearing concerned, he asked, "So what did happen to you then?"

I didn't know how to answer. I could have just lied, but when I looked into his eyes, I didn't want to. There was something about Emerson's soft brown eyes that made me want to pour my heart out to him.

"I busted my lip," I replied, taking the easy way out before changing the subject by asking, "Now why do you wanna get to know me better?"

Emerson flashed a quick smile before saying, "Well you're not hard to look at," as my face started turning red he shared, "I see you at school all the time and I... I'm kind of curious about you. You always look, I don't know, like you need a hug."

Tilting my head to the side, I asked, "You wanna give me a hug?"

He shrugged before he stepped right in front of me, taking my question as an offer.

Emerson wrapped his arms around me. As he held me tight, I couldn't believe the feeling it invoked. In the fifteen years I had been alive, I'd held hands, been pushed, kissed, shoved, felt up once, and slapped, but never once hugged. That one hug was all it took. I was in love. Not the heart pounding I can't wait to get you alone love. The kind of love that makes you feel safe and secure. Leaning my cheek against his chest, I hugged him back.

I was a little sad when he let go.

Trying to pretend the hug wasn't as important to me as it truly was, I laughed, "So, now you've hugged me. Feel better?"

Emerson's smile was sweet as he concluded, "I think we both do."

I couldn't stop myself from smiling. The thought occurred to me that aside from their money and position, the Roberts' were really nice people. Feeling bad now for thinking his mother was a little off; I decided to talk to Emerson about her.

"Your mother is really nice."

With a curious expression, he questioned, "My mother?"

Nodding, I explained, "Well, I just met her and she offered to have me over for dinner on my birthday."

A slight smirk crossed Emerson's face as he informed, "She must like you. Just so you know, that's a pretty big deal. My mother is always very polite, but she will put someone in their place quick if they don't meet her expectations."

"She said I was lovely," I shared, feeling proud of myself.

Smiling wide this time, Emerson asked, "Would you want to come back over, tomorrow?"

"Sure but I have to ask my father."

"If you can I'll come and pick you up."

I nodded at him, hoping my father would let me come over again.

The rest of the evening seemed to fly by as we finished our game. On the way home, I thought about how different Emerson was from Hert.

Breaking my train of thought, Emerson asked, "Why are you so quiet?"

Before I could think my answer through, I replied, "Sorry, I was thinking about Hert."

"Oh."

He sounded so disappointed, I felt the need to explain myself.

"I had a lot of fun with you, it's just... He's having some problems and ..." before I could finish, Emerson broke in, "Because his father left?"

I was startled for a moment, then I reminded myself, in a small town everyone knows everyone's business.

"I guess," I answered.

Almost apologizing, he shared, "I heard my father tell my mother the other night."

Wondering why it was any of the Roberts' business, I asked, "What did he say?"

"That he had left and that they should see what they could do to help."

Nodding, I tried to pretend I wasn't bothered by strangers talking about my friend.

We reached my house and even though I assured him it wasn't necessary, Emerson walked me to the front door, and then into my house.

Glancing at my father, Emerson greeted, "Mr. Cantinelli," with a slight nod.

My father remained at the kitchen table, stating, "Emerson."

Very politely, Emerson asked, "May I pick Rennillia up tomorrow, around noon?"

Nodding, my father replied, "Of Course you can, my boy."

"Thank you, sir."

Emerson turned to leave. He wasn't even a foot away when my father pointed and mouthed, 'walk him out.' Giving a sarcastic smile, I complied.

Outside my front door, I stopped, saying, "I really did have a good time."

Emerson smiled at me before he agreed, "I did too."

As I watched him walk to his car, it occurred to me that although I had a great time, I missed Hert. When I walked back inside, my short mental debate on whether to sneak over and see Hert, was decided the moment my father spoke.

"Emerson is who you should associate yourself with, unlike that boy. Be home by this time tomorrow."

Somehow, I managed to keep my mouth shut and smile at my father as I headed to my room. Even if I had thought it was a bad idea, I still would have gone to visit Hert after that.

How was Emerson 'my boy' and Hert 'that boy'? My father's logic made me sick. As quick as I could, I pulled my dress off, and threw it across the room. How perfect it must be for my father to have a daughter the same age as the Roberts' son. Instead of allowing me the one friend I always had, he was associating me with the 'right people'. I pulled on a pair of jeans and a t-shirt. Grabbing my shoes out of my closet, I climbed out of my window.

Practically running, I made it to Hert's window in record time. I didn't see him at first. Waiting patiently outside until finally he stepped back into his room, I tapped on his window.

"Hey," he greeted, opening his window.

I noticed a strange expression on his face as I climbed in, saying, "Hey."

Appearing nervous, Hert took a step back, asking, "What's going on?"

Confused as to why he was acting this way, I replied, "Not much, I thought I'd come by and see you."

Nodding, he sat down on the edge of his bed.

"So, how is it with just you and your mom?" I asked, expecting him to be happy.

Scowling at me, he snapped, "Fine. What are you doing here?"

"You know what? I really don't know," I blurted as I turned and climbed back out of his window.

Infuriated by Hert's lack of enthusiasm, I started my walk home.

About half way to my house, I heard footsteps quickly approaching. I glanced back and saw Hert catching up to me. Determined to ignore him, I kept walking.

In a semi-hushed shout, Hert called, "Renni."

Quickly turning towards him, I blurted, "What?"

"It's one thirty in the morning."

Giving him a stupid look, I spouted, "Oh, I'm sorry, I didn't know it was past your bedtime," before turning away and continuing my walk home.

I could hear him snap, "Next time, stay your ass at home."
Fighting the urge to turn and yell at him, I walked faster. The closer I got to my house the angrier I was at him.

The contrast between Hert, and who I could only assume was a new friend, Emerson, was clear. Climbing back in my window, mumbling mean things about Hert, I really didn't think about how late it was, but still, did he have to be such a jerk? Walking through my room and into my bathroom, I glanced at the mirror and realized I'd better wash my face and shower before bed.

After my shower, I curled up under my comforter and closed my eyes. Thinking about the no-dinner, dinner, at Emerson's, I wondered if it was a fluke or if it would be as much fun tomorrow as it was tonight.

Chapter 4

I woke up with less than an hour to get ready. Dragging myself out of bed and into the kitchen, I started thinking of ways to get out of my afternoon with Emerson. It wasn't that I disliked being there. Before I fell asleep, I was almost excited to go back, but the idea of going today was making me anxious. Thinking of excuses to bail on my plans, I watched my father sit down at the table.

"Aren't you going with Emerson today?"

Nodding, I answered, "Yes sir."

With a harsh tone, my father uttered, "Too much to ask for you to look nice two days in a row, I guess."

"Guess so," I spouted as I stood up.

Grabbing my arm before I could walk away, my father pulled me against the side of the table.

He stared directly in the eyes, warning, "Boys like Emerson don't waste their time on girls that give it away."

Well, of course, girls that wear dresses and fix their hair never sleep around.

I smiled a sarcastic smile and assured, "I'll try to control myself."

Pulling me farther against the table, he snarled, "Big mouth, saccente."

Hoping I could get myself in enough trouble to stay home, I snapped, "What else am I gonna do with him? He has a girlfriend."

Justified in his rage, my father jumped to his feet, jerking me around to face him.

"So, more than your mouth is smart after all."

"What?"

Holding my forearm so tight my fingers were going numb, he answered, "That's quite a plan. There's no way he would want you for anything else." As the hurt from his accusation invaded my self-esteem, he continued, "Do whatever you need to, but make it count. Otherwise you're just another whore."

He slowly released his grip when there was a knock at the door.

I ran to my room before my father could see me cry. In my effort to back out of my plans, I somehow got the okay to trap Emerson into I don't know what. I felt as if my father was saying things, as he often did, to make me feel bad about myself; however the fact that he actually thought I was capable of such a thing really hurt. I quickly brushed through my hair, and pulled it up before dressing in jeans, and a t-shirt. Sliding my shoes on, I walked back into the kitchen to meet Emerson.

I did my best to smile as Emerson greeted, "Are you ready?"

Nodding, I refused to look at my father as I stated, "I'll be home later."

It took all my strength not to say anything back when my father cheered, "You kids have fun."

I was somewhere between nausea and disgust as I walked out of the door Emerson opened for me.

A few minutes into our ride, I realized, I should have brought a sweater. Quickly crossing my arms, I tried to hide the purple that was spreading across my forearm before Emerson noticed it.

"Are you cold?" he thoughtfully asked.

The sound of his voice comforted me as I replied, "A little."

Reaching into the backseat, he grabbed a jacket and handed it to me.

"Thank you."

"Are you feeling okay?"

Nodding, I replied, "I'm fine."

Silence filled the car for a moment before Emerson shared, "I forgot to tell you last night, I have a date tonight. I'll have to bring you home before seven."

Suddenly the things my father said filled my mind as I questioned, "Why did you invite me back then?"

His eyes were apologetic.

"I wanted to see you again."

Shaking my head, I blurted, "For what?"

With a confused expression that quickly turned compassionate, he assured, "I like you. You're... Well, you seem more real than most people, and I thought we were friends." The sincerity in his tone made me feel guilty for expecting the worst of him.

The rest of the drive was silent.

When we arrived at his house, he opened the car door, and then the back door for me.

"Should I tell your parents hello?" I asked as we walked into the kitchen.

Shaking his head, Emerson informed, "They're at an event."

With a slow nod, I asked, "Is it okay that I'm here?"

Smiling, he rolled his eyes. "Yes, Rennillia. Do you want to hang out in my room?"

Shrugging slightly, I replied, "Sure."

I followed him up the stairs and into a long hallway full of doors.

Emerson opened the first door to our right. Allowing me to step in first, he quickly walked around me and straight to his dresser. I looked around, noticing trophies, and various photos of Emerson. Everything inside his room matched perfectly to the black and gray bedspread.

"Nice."

As I continued to look around he pulled a long sleeve shirt out of his dresser drawer.

"This might be more comfortable than that jacket, if you're still cold."

Nodding as I took it, something occurred to me.

"If we're friends, you have to stop calling me Rennillia."

With a slight smile, he asked, "What do you want me to call you then?"

Smiling back, I answered, "Ren, is good."

"Okay, Ren, I know you just got here, but do you want to come back tomorrow?"

After taking a moment to think, I declined.

"I was gonna try to go see Hert."

He appeared a bit disappointed as he asked, "What do you want to do today then?"

Shrugging, I questioned, "What do usually do on a Saturday afternoon?"

"I usually practice, free throws and my jump shot but we don't have..." he started before I broke in, "Okay, I'll play."

With a speculative stare, Emerson shared, "I already saw your arm. So, you don't have to have a heatstroke hiding it from me," as he took his shirt from me.

Unsure of what to say, I nodded, hoping he wouldn't ask any questions.

We started out taking turns shooting the basketball on a half court on the other side of the garage. Then, after a hysterical attempt at one on one, we sat down on the court.

Scooting close, Emerson placed his arm around my shoulders. "I don't think I've ever had this much fun with a girl before."

With a smirk, I informed, "I think you should change the type of girls you hang out with then."

He let out a light chuckle before his expression turned serious.

"Do you want to tell me what happened?"

Sitting there with him, I really did. The feel of his arm around me made me feel safe. It was almost as if being close to him would keep any bad or hurtful thing away.

Taking a breath, I replied, "Not really."

"Okay then, can I ask you something?"

"You can ask me anything you want, but I can't guarantee I'll answer you."

"Is it true your father caught you and Scott in bed together?"

I couldn't help finding the humor in his question as I replied, "No," with a laugh.

His eyes questioned my honesty.

"Hert was at my house without permission, and my father did come home and catch us, but we were in the kitchen washing dishes."

"Man when you break the rules you go all out," he teased.

"I know. I'm such a deviant. And just so you know, I'm friends with Hert, not friendly friends, just friends."

Emerson gave me a strange look before shaking his head and laughing at me.

As Emerson's laughter subsided, his eyes appeared more thoughtful. He removed his arm from around my shoulders and stood up. I took the hand he held out to me and stood up also. We walked back into his house, still holding hands. Much like his hug from the night before, the feel of his hand around mine made me feel secure and protected.

When we sat down, on the couch in the living room, Emerson replaced his arm around my shoulders, saying, "Do you want to watch a movie?"

"Sure, but can I ask you a favor?"

As he nodded, I asked, "You don't have to, but since you have a date, and I don't have to be back until midnight, do you think you could drop me at Hert's? Then, pick me up and bring me home after?"

Emerson gave me an uncomfortable look.

"It's not that I mind, I don't want you to get into trouble."

"Is that a yes?" I asked, adding, "If it is, I can come back tomorrow."

I could tell he was conflicted as he sighed, "Alright."

Smiling wide, I leaned over and hugged him.

On the way to Hert's, I thought about how nice it would be to spend to day with the two of them. They were so different, and although I really liked spending time with Emerson, I missed Hert at the same time.

"Would it be okay if Hert came with me tomorrow?" I asked, glancing over at Emerson.

With a light smile, Emerson replied, "If that's what you want."

Nodding, I smiled, incredibly pleased with the idea.

We pulled up in front of Hert's house and Emerson quickly opened his door and dashed over to my side. As he opened my door, I shook my head and smiled.

"You really don't have to be so formal with me," I assured, stepping out of his car.

He placed his arm around my shoulders as he insisted, "I'm not being formal, it's polite."

I gave him a brief hug.

"Thanks, and don't forget to come back and get me."

"Eleven thirty, okay," he stated as I darted to Hert's font door.

It took several minutes for Hert to answer after I knocked on his door. He looked upset.

"Are you okay?" I questioned, taking a step back.
Without answering, Hert opened the door wider, allowing me to walk in. Glancing around, I didn't see his mother anywhere. Unsure of what I expected, I did think his house would be happier with his father gone.

"Is it okay if I hang out here for a while?"
Nodding, Hert walked to his room as I followed. He closed the door behind us and sat down on the edge of his bed.

Narrowing his eyes at me, he questioned, "Does your father know you're here?"

Shaking my head, I shared, "I was at Emerson's and he has a date, so I asked him to drop me off here. He's picking me up at eleven thirty."

"Guess the dinner went well." Hert snapped.

Irritated by his attitude, I griped, "Do you want me to leave?"
He just sat there staring at me.

"Okay, then, don't be like that. Emerson is really nice."

"Yea, I bet he is."

Exhaling loudly, I informed, "Yea, he is," before changing the subject. "How is it with just you and your mom?"
Hert's expression changed as he scowled and shrugged his shoulders.

I sat down on his bed watching him carefully. He didn't turn towards me or even move. Thinking of Emerson, and how good it felt for him to hug me, I stretched out on my side and tapped Hert on the back.

As he turned to look at me, I offered, "You wanna hug?"

"No thanks." Hert replied, shaking his head as he cracked a smile.

Scooting farther onto the bed, he questioned, "Roberts was nice to you?"

Nodding, I looked up at him, sharing, "He really is nice. I didn't think I would like him, but it's kinda hard not to."

Changing the subject, I started to say, "So, tomorrow…" before he stopped me. "Is Sunday."

"Well, if you don't have plans, come with me to Emerson's."

Hert rolled onto his back. "I'd rather talk about your birthday."

Confused, I asked, "Instead of coming with me tomorrow?"

Mirroring my look, he questioned, "Do you want to do something for your birthday or not?"

Raising an eyebrow, I teased, "Are you asking me out?"

Hert looked at me like I was stupid. Brushing off the fact that he found the idea so offensive, I got back on point.

"I think Mrs. Roberts is having a dinner for me, but after I can figure out a way for us to do something."

Sitting back up, he shrugged off my suggestion.

We spent the rest of the evening in silence. Emerson arrived right on time to get me. Hert stayed in his room when I left. Frustrated there was no winning with him, in the five minutes it took to drive from Hert's house to mine, I decided he was feeling left out. After Emerson dropped me off, I politely blew off my father's comments on the evening and went to my room. It was after midnight and even though I knew he would be irritated, I snuck back over to Hert's and told him happy birthday.

Chapter 5

Between school, Emerson's, and sneaking out to see Hert, the days passed quickly and before I knew it, I was sixteen. My father actually gave me an excellent birthday present, by going out of town. He made me a hair appointment before he left of course, which was nice too. My plan was to get up, get my hair done, have dinner at the Roberts' house, and then have Emerson drop me at Hert's.

After rolling out of bed, I skipped to the kitchen, ready to start my day. To my surprise, there was a small box on the kitchen table next to my plate. Smiling at the box, I sat down and opened it. My eyes instantly welled up with tears when I saw what was inside. It was a thin gold bracelet with tiny emeralds staggered around it.

My mother sat down at the table with me, sharing, "It was your Grandma Nillia's."

Smiling up at her, I replied, "I remember. Thank you."

"Hurry up now, you don't want to be late for your appointment."

I ran my finger down the bracelet before sliding it out of the box, and clasping it around my wrist. I couldn't believe it was mine. It was the only thing I remembered about my grandmother aside from being named after her.

With my trip into town to get my hair done out of the way, I stood in front of the mirror in my room. Looking at my reflection, I smiled at the pink dress I was wearing before lifting my wrist and watching my bracelet sparkle as it slid against my arm. Wondering if my mother knew how truly important her gift was to me, I decided to thank her again.

I walked into the kitchen and sat down next to her, saying, "Mom, this is the best present ever."

I noticed her eyes start to water before she nodded, stood up, and walked to her room. Thinking to myself, 'well then, okay,' I got up from the table and headed to the front door. Deciding to wait for Emerson outside, I leaned against my front door.

Emerson arrived right on time, looking sharp in his suit jacket and slacks. He opened the passenger side door and waited for me get in. Smiling, I walked to his car.

"Happy Birthday, Ren," he greeted as I slid into his car.

Shaking my head at the moment, I offered, "You look really nice."

"So do you," he shared, getting back into the car.

Reaching over, he held my hand, asking, "Is Hert coming?"

"We're going somewhere, later tonight."

With a serious expression, Emerson questioned, "Aren't you worried about getting in trouble?"

With a slight laugh, I assured, "I either will or I won't, it's not something I worry about."

"I worry about it."

Letting go of his hand, I turned to face him.

"Look, it's not like I'm sneaking out to do wrong. Hert has been my friend for the last sixteen years, and it's not fair that my father woke up one morning and decided we shouldn't be friends anymore."

"I'm sorry, I wasn't trying to upset you."

"You didn't," I snapped, before quickly changing the subject. "Is your girlfriend coming to dinner?"

Shaking his head, Emerson informed, "She broke up with me last night."

Pouting on his behalf, I shared, "For the record, I never liked her, you can do way better."

"Thank you, I know," Emerson replied.

I started to laugh, wondering if he said 'I know' to the fact that he could do better, or that I never liked her.

After giving me a few strange looks, he focused on the road. Sure he thought I was crazy, I couldn't help myself. The thought of Emerson thinking he could do better was so unlike him, I found it funny. I meant what I said though, I couldn't stand her, and he could do better. He was so thoughtful and considerate of other people it seemed like he never really thought about himself.

When we arrived at his house, he pulled around to the back driveway.

"Got your eye on anyone new?"

Emerson appeared flustered as he reminded, "We just broke up."

Unhappy with the idea of him actually missing her, I coaxed, "Oh, come on."

With a slight shrug, Emerson admitted, "There is one girl. I'm not sure she feels that way about me."

"Why wouldn't she?" I questioned before assuring, "You're sweet, thoughtful, and incredibly handsome."

"You think so?"

Nodding vigorously, I confirmed, "Yes, I do."

"So?"

"So, maybe she doesn't realize how great you are. You need to exercise some of that Roberts' charm and win her over, because any girl would be lucky to have you."

With a nod he opened the back door and we walked into the kitchen.

Sitting at the Roberts' massive dining room table, I quietly ate. Mr. Roberts was seated at the head with Mrs. Roberts on his right, and Emerson and I to his left. After birthday wishes and a few uncomfortable questions concerning my plans for the future, I appreciated the silence.

Out of nowhere, Mrs. Roberts asked, "Your friend couldn't make it to dinner?"

Caught off guard, I blurted, "Ma'am?"

"Emerson said you were bringing a friend."

Wishing Hert would have come, I replied, "Oh, no ma'am, he couldn't make it."

Giving me a suspicious look, she questioned, "He?"

I gave her a polite nod before answering,

"Yes ma'am, I wanted Hert... Scott Herterand to come, but..."

She quickly cut me off, stating, "I was not aware the two of you were close."

Wondering if she had a problem with Hert, I recalled Emerson saying his parents had discussed Hert's family.

Careful with my tone, I replied, "I've been friends with him my whole life."

To my surprise, Mr. Roberts chimed in.

"I am sure if he is a friend of Rennillia's, he is a fine young man." I slowly smiled at him as he assured, "He will be welcome here, anytime," in a firm tone.

Keeping her tone short, Mrs. Roberts replied, "I wasn't implying otherwise."

As Mr. and Mrs. Roberts stared at each other, I wondered if I had just witnessed an argument between the two of them. Since they were so polite, it was hard to tell. Arguments at my house were nothing like this.

Once dinner was over, Mr. and Mrs. Roberts wished me a happy birthday for the second time before heading upstairs. I couldn't help feeling a little sad, sitting on the living room couch with Emerson. As nice as Mrs. Roberts was to me, it was very clear she wasn't fond of Hert. I knew his father was horrible, but that wasn't his fault.

I decided to question Emerson about it, just in case I was being a little over protective, and misunderstood.

"Why doesn't your mother like Hert?"

Giving me a confused expression, he replied, "I think she was expecting a girl when I told her you were bringing a friend."

"Oh..." I sighed, feeling a little better.

Emerson placed his arm around my shoulders.

"Thank you for spending your birthday with me."

Leaning the side of my head onto his shoulder, I looked up at him.

"I really like hanging out with you."

His brown eyes were soft as he questioned, "Really?"

"I'm glad we're friends." I nodded with a smile.

Nodding back, Emerson kissed my forehead.

"Me too."

Sitting with Emerson was comforting. There was something about being close to him that made me, for lack of a better word, sleepy. Emerson was like the comforter on my bed that I curled up in when I was upset. Thoughts of being able to curl up with him made me wish he could stay the night with me. Thinking about how I could make that happen, I noticed it was getting late.

Hert was waiting on the curb in front of his house, in his mother's car, when Emerson and I pulled up. Patting his shoulder, I gave him a smile before hopping out of the car. Giving him a little wave as he pulled away, I hoped I hadn't hurt his feelings by not letting him open my door.

"Well, I'm yours for the rest of the night," I laughed, smiling wide at Hert as I slid in on the passenger side.

Hert smiled back at first, then narrowed his eyes at me.

"Why are you dressed like that?"

Making a face at him, I snapped, "Some people think I look nice."

"I didn't say you didn't look nice, I asked why you were dressed like that."

"It's my birthday and some people think that sorta thing is special."

Glaring at me, he questioned, "Since when do you dress up for your birthday?"

With a slight smirk, I replied, "Didn't you know? I'm a lovely young lady."

Raising an eyebrow, Hert laughed, "Yea, and I'm a gentleman."

As Hert and I laughed at each other, we headed out to the pond.

At the pond, we threw rocks in the water and a few at each other before sitting down on a blanket. Thinking of all the times he and I had been out here, I realized this was the first time it was just us. Giving Hert a little shove, I smiled when he shoved me back.

Without looking at me, Hert quietly asked, "Are you going out with Roberts?"

Shocked, I blurted, "No."

Giving me an unpleasant expression, he accused, "Then why are you spending so much time with him?"

"We're friends."

He shook his head at me, disagreeing, "Yea, right now."

Infuriated with him, I snapped, "What the hell is that supposed to mean?"

"You think Roberts wants you as a friend?"

Raising my voice, I replied, "Yea, and you think you know everything, but you don't."

Turning to face me, Hert griped, "And you're stupid if you think Roberts just wants to be friends."

Shrinking back a little, I felt stupid. Not because of Emerson, I did believe we were really friends, because Hert had a way of making me feel bad.

I laid back thinking Hert should have come with me to Emerson's, then he would see. Was it really so strange for someone like Emerson to want to be friends with me? I had only known him for a little while, but I could tell he needed a real friend. His parents were hardly home, his stupid now ex-girlfriend was so fake, and all anyone else seemed to care about was that he was a 'Roberts'. As I looked up at Hert I noticed his frustrated expression as he stared down at me.

"I wish you were more like Emerson," I shared before closing my eyes.

A long moment passed before I opened my eyes and heard him say, "We're not little kids anymore Renni, you don't have to be here with me if that's not what you want."

With a loud sigh, I griped, "You're such an ass."

"Oh, I almost forgot."

As Hert ignored my comment on his greatest personality trait, he jumped up and walked to the car.

He made his way back carrying a small Styrofoam container. Sitting up, I watched him place it in front of me.

"What's this?"

With a slight smile, he replied, "Open it."

I opened the container and found a square piece of tiramisu.

"Thank you." I smiled at my cake first, and then at Hert.

He smiled back and handed me a plastic fork.

"I hope it's still good, I picked it up this afternoon."

"You wanna share?" I asked holding it between us.

He nodded and I used the fork to cut the cake in half.

As we scooped up our halves, I raised mine, declaring, "Sixteen down, two to go."

Hert gave a slight nod before touching his piece of cake to mine.

Chapter 6

After my birthday, Hert agreed to come to Emerson's with me. Hert and Emerson were polar opposites, but together, they seemed to balance each other out. Of course, Mr. Roberts liked Hert. He stood up tall and used the word sir a lot. Mrs. Roberts, on the other hand, gave the impression she was tolerating his presence in her house, but was still very polite to him. I didn't care because it was like having the best of both worlds, and the best part was, I didn't have to sneak around to see Hert anymore. The three of us were always together before school, after school and on the weekends. When summer came it was even better. I was hardly at home, which was a big plus for me. My Father was happy I was at the Roberts', and I was happy to spend all day everyday with Hert and Emerson.

When our junior year started, Emerson picked me up every morning before we swung by Hert's to get him. Emerson had a new girlfriend, and Hert still saw Carmella, but aside from that, they were mine. Everything seemed perfect and I couldn't imagine my life being better. Even my father seemed content. It was possible seeing him as little as possible was the reason. However, his latest investment seemed to be behind his better mood. He even bought me a little car. Surprising me one day after school, with the condition of to school and back home of course. Things were going so well, I stopped counting the days until I turned eighteen and just enjoyed myself. Until the night I woke up hearing my father yelling.

Unsure of what was happening I rolled out of bed, and crept into the kitchen. My mother was sitting at the kitchen table crying, and my father was shouting and cursing in Italian. I wasn't fluent in any foreign language, but I could pick out the words 'off limits' and 'forbidden'. As I tried to listen without being involved, my father noticed me. Before I could make it back to my room, I heard him call me.

"Rennillia!"

Slowly walking towards him, I whispered, "Sir?"

"I told you! Didn't I? I warned you!"

Confused, I shook my head at him.

"That bastard and his whore mother... They killed him."

"What?" I blurted, unable to understand what had happened.

Grabbing hold of my face, my father growled, "I catch you anywhere near them and I'll beat you 'til you can't see straight."

His threat provoked me to jerk away as I spouted, "I don't even know what you're talking about."

He raised his hand then to my surprise, he turned and stormed off to his room.

Looking up from the table, my mother wiped her eyes and explained, "They found Charles dead in his motel room." Stunned, I shook my head at her as she added, "He drank himself to death."

Not knowing what to do, I ran to my room.

Pacing back and forth, I wanted to go see Hert. I wondered if he knew and if he did, did he even care? I was so angry with my father. Hert's father was horrible when he was alive, and now that he was gone, Hert and his mother were still getting blamed. Unable to stay in my room, doing nothing, I locked my door and decided to go see if Hert was okay. Throwing on jeans and a t-shirt, I climbed out of my window and ran to Hert's house.

Peering into his room through the window, I didn't see him. I decided to wait for him, sliding his window open and climbing in.

As I sat on the edge of his bed, I heard Mrs. Herterand cry out, "It's my fault."

Hert yelled, "Stop saying that."

Guessing I caught the end of their conversation, I jumped a little when his door swung open.

I could tell he was angry as he slammed his door, and fussed, "Go home."

"Hert, I just..." I started to say before he snapped, "I don't care. Go home."

"Please, I heard what happened."

"I don't give a damn, get out."

I refused to believe he didn't want me there as I stood up and reached out to him.

"Look at me."

Hert grabbed me by my shoulders. Jerking me forward, he leaned close, gritting his teeth at me.

"Get the hell out."

Shrugging his hands off of me, I slapped him.

"Stop it."

His eyes were filled with a harsh realization as he shook his head.

"I don't want you here."

His words were worse than if he had slapped me back. Nodding at him, I turned and went home. I didn't bother to change back into my pajamas. I just curled up in my comforter and laid there feeling sad.

A few hours passed before I heard my father yelling again. Covering my head with my pillow, I sighed when my door knob started to turn.

"Why is this door locked?"

Swiftly jumping up and unlocking it, I lied. "I was changing."

My father narrowed his eyes at me, he knew I was lying, but what could he say, I had jeans and a t-shirt on.

"No school for the rest of the week."

Ordinarily, that would have been a happy thought, but since it meant no Hert or Emerson, I argued.

"Why not?"

"Just do what you're told."

Holding my head high in defiance, I stated, "No."

His eyes were wild with fury as he shoved me back, shouting, "You are gonna know your place."

Before I could do or say anything else, he kicked my leg out from underneath me. I fell to the floor. Covering my face with my arms, I thought of that first night at the Roberts' when Emerson hugged me. The memory helped my will remain intact as my father did everything in his power to make me 'know my place'.

Chapter 7

As it turned out, I welcomed missing the next few days of school. Who would have thought my little hairbrush could cause such damage? When used as a tool of instruction, however, it left purplish blue splotches all over my body.

Preparing myself for Mr. Herterand's funeral, I dressed in grey slacks and a long black sweater. Heading out of my room, I slowly made my way to the kitchen. My father didn't apologize for overreacting when I told him no, but he did have my mother bring breakfast, lunch and dinner to my room over the last two days. That was his way of admitting his latest attempt to correct my behavior was a little uncalled for. In a way, I understood. He was upset his friend had died and to be fair, I did sneak over to Hert's whether he knew it or not.

Breakfast was on the table when I walked in. My father was seated at the table, and my mother stood at the stove as usual.

Pushing the chair next to him slightly, my father offered, "Sit and eat."

Staying still, I replied, "I'm not hungry."

With a slight grunt, he finished his breakfast before leaving the table to finish getting dressed.

"It means a lot to your father that you're going," my mother whispered.

Nodding at her, I thought, 'like I had a choice'.

Making my way over to her, I asked, "Why aren't you going?"

Without answering my question, she shook her head, saying, "You should get your hair done more often. Then you wouldn't have to pull it up all the time."

Before I could question her again, my father walked back into the room and it was time to go.

On the way to the funeral, neither of us said a word. I knew my father was thinking mean things about Hert and Mrs. Herterand by the way he would squint his eyes, and then mumble to himself. Leaning my head back, I closed my eyes and wondered how Hert was doing. The last time I saw him, it was clear, the answer to that question was 'not so good'.

Far more people attended Charles Herterand's funeral than I would have thought. Although we sat on the front row, we were all the way on the other side from Hert and his mother. The service was short, which was a relief, because my father blocked my view of Hert and I really wanted to see him.

When everyone stood and made their way to the front to offer condolences, my father took my arm and led me in the opposite direction. I knew why. My father didn't pretend. He was the type of man that would refuse such a thing, if he deemed it beneath him. I started to get upset to the point that tears were filling my eyes. Then, I saw Mr. Roberts walking towards us from the back row. Both my father and I stopped.

Giving me a slight nod, Mr. Roberts greeted, "Rennillia," before staring at my father. "Are you leaving?"

Letting go of my arm, my father snapped, "The service is over."

Mr. Roberts took a step closer to my father and narrowed his eyes at him.

"You're not going to offer your condolences?"

Raising his voice, my father snapped, "Not to them."

Mr. Roberts' tone turned angry as he questioned, "You have watched the boy grow up and you aren't even going to go shake his hand?"

Without waiting for a reply, Mr. Roberts stood tall and glared at my father.

"Rennillia, would you like to walk with me?" Mr. Roberts asked, softening his expression.

I was so shocked, I couldn't respond.

Luckily, I didn't have to. My father walked away without a word, leaving me there with Mr. Roberts. Giving me a reassuring smile, Mr. Roberts headed towards the front as I followed. Out of respect, I stayed at his side but kept my pace a step behind. I started to feel anxious the closer we got to Hert. Mr. Roberts went first. I watched him give Mrs. Herterand, who was standing behind Hert, a thoughtful look before holding his hand out.

Hert greeted, "Mr. Roberts," taking his hand with a firm shake.

"If there is anything I can do, please do not hesitate," Mr. Roberts assured.

With a nod, Hert accepted. "Yes sir."

"I will give you two a moment."

Mr. Roberts glanced at Mrs. Herterand, again, before stepping off to the side.

I walked around Hert to Mrs. Herterand and hugged her, saying, "I'm sorry for your loss."

At first, she seemed shocked, then she patted my back and breathed, "Thank you."

Glaring down at me, Hert's expression was serious. I couldn't think of a single thing to say. Forcing a soft smile, I shrugged my shoulder at him. As I started to walk away, he caught my arm.

Leaning to my ear, he whispered, "Don't come by."

I couldn't bring myself to look at him as I nodded.

Meeting up with Mr. Roberts, I followed him to his car. The driver opened the door for us and motioned for me to go first. Sliding in the back seat, I folded my hands onto my lap. My mind was racing with how sad Mrs. Herterand appeared, the way Hert looked, and my father leaving me with Mr. Roberts. Staring at my hands, I pretended I wasn't on the verge of bursting into tears.

"Are you alright?" Mr. Roberts asked with a thoughtful tone.

"Yes sir."

"Would you like to go home?"

His tone was so smooth, I felt like it required an explanation, "No sir, my father won't be happy to see me."

Tilting his head to the side, Mr. Roberts inquired, "What does your father have against Scott?"

Looking up from my hands, I replied, "He isn't Emerson."

With a slight nod, he focused his attention outside the window.

"Emerson is very fond of you."

"I like him a lot too," I assured, wondering where this was going.

The conversation took a strange turn as Mr. Roberts imparted, "Life is full of difficult decisions. You should be proud of the way you handled yourself today."

Unsure of what he was referring to, I questioned, "Sir?"

He drew in a deep breath as he replied, "You're different than I expected you to be. I am glad my son has you in his life."

Watching him carefully, I caught a glimpse of what appeared to be pain, or maybe sorrow in his expression.

"Mr. Roberts, are you okay?"

Thrown off by the smirk on his face, apparently he found my question humorous.

"By the time you get to be where I am, there is no way to answer that question."

Nodding, I looked back down at my hands, feeling like I was missing something.

At the Roberts' house, I was happy to find Emerson already home from school. Mr. Roberts informed us that he had business to attend to and would return later. Mrs. Roberts was at one of her Society functions and would also be gone for a while. As Emerson and I headed to his room, I looked forward to seeing how his day went and catch up on anything I missed over the last few days.

Sitting on the edge of his bed, I asked, "How's the new one?"

Shaking his head at me, Emerson corrected, "Emma is fine."

Laughing a little, I shared, "If she stays with you for more than a few weeks, I'll call her by her name. Until then, she's the new one."

With a slight laugh in return, he questioned, "Why did you stay home from school?"

Shrugging off his question, I glanced away from him.

"Your father said you were sick."

Remaining silent, I slipped my shoes off and folded my legs in front of myself on the bed.

Emerson's eyes were sympathetic as he swore, "You can tell me."

His offer made me uneasy.

"Tell you what?"

"If something's wrong."

"What would be wrong?"

"I could tell you what I think, but I don't want you to be upset with me."

Without being able to stop myself, I started to cry.

Everything that happened up to this moment seemed to weigh heavily on me. Hert, my father, Hert's father, it seemed as though nothing existed outside of pain and sorrow. I was mourning a life I never cared about. One whose end provoked the heavy hand of my father, brought about the self-imposed isolation of my friend, and all I could do was cry.

Emerson wrapped his arms around me tight at first. Still sore from not knowing my place, my whole body tensed up. Loosening his hold, Emerson's arms gently draped over me. Lightly patting the side of my head, he sat there letting me curl up onto him. As I let every held back tear loose, I thought it wasn't Emerson who needed me. I needed him.

Chapter 8

Three months after Mr. Herterand's funeral, things seemed to go back to normal, but everything was changing. My little stunt at the funeral, in my father's words, cost me the use of my car. It didn't matter though, Emerson just picked me up for school instead. Hert drove himself and met us in the parking lot every morning. Aside from that, Hert stopped by Emerson's occasionally, but never stayed very long. I wondered if maybe Carmella was the reason, and that would explain why he didn't want me coming by anymore, but seeing as he never took her out in public, that more than likely wasn't it. Maybe his father's death affected him more than anyone realized. Emerson was on new girl number three for the year, and she was something else. In fact, Mrs. Roberts, who was always composed and proper, had a hard time tolerating her. I even heard her use the words low class in reference to Miss Number Three, which was odd because her family was very well to-do. Not understanding what Emerson saw in her, I decided she put out and that would account for the goofy way he mooned over her. Other than that, she didn't interfere with my time with him, so I didn't put much thought into her.

In the car on the way home from school, I sat on the passenger side pouting. Emerson was failing miserably at making me feel better.

"They're just looking."

Shaking my head at him, I argued, "Your mother didn't make it sound like they were just looking."

With a heavy sigh, he insisted, "Her family is from there and they've been talking about purchasing an estate there for years."

"Spain, Emerson. They are looking for a house in Spain," I fussed before reminding, "That's a whole other country."

Giving me a slight reality check, Emerson replied, "I know. I've been there before."

'Oh, that's right', for a minute there I forgot who I was talking to', I thought as we pulled up in front of my house. While I waited for him to open my door, I had to admit what my real problem was. As soon as Emerson opened my door, I slid my arms under his and hugged him tight.

"I don't want you to move away."

"They're just looking," he assured, hugging me back.
After nodding into his chest, I pulled away, and walked to my front door.

Once inside, I headed straight for my room. Barely glancing toward the kitchen, I saw my father sitting at the table. My mother was nowhere to be seen, so I assumed I was in charge of dinner. I threw my books and purse on my bed before heading back to make dinner.

My father sat in his usual spot, but as I got closer, I noticed a bottle of liquor and a glass in front of him. It wasn't unusual for my father to drink. Chianti was his drink of choice with dinner. From the time I was twelve my father allowed me a glass of wine with Sunday dinner. It really consisted of a wine glass with the bottom barely filled, two sips at the most if I stretched it. This was different. It was a bottle of Nocino.

When he noticed me, my father slid the glass to the spot next to him, and filled the bottom.

His voice was low as he offered, "Have a drink."
I'd never seen my father like this.

"Where's mom?"

Motioning to the back of the house before sliding the glass closer to me, he ordered, "Sit."
He took a long swig directly from the bottle as I quietly sat next to him. Since I had no idea what was going on, I assumed keeping my mouth shut was the best route.

Narrowing his eyes at me, he questioned, "Too good to drink with your own father?"
I wrapped my hand around the glass. He wasn't slurring, but his motion and speech were so calm and slow, I knew he was drunk.

As I took a sip, he shared, "Me and Charles used to drink this."

The liquor wasn't good, but it wasn't bad either. I quickly downed what was left in my glass, thinking, if I had to listen to this man glorify Hert's father then I definitely needed to drink.

After refilling the bottom of my glass, my father took another sip from the bottle, mumbling, "Not me."

"Sir?"

With a heavy sigh, he rambled, "Margaret, she's sad." Then with an eerie smile, he added, "Not me."

I downed the rest of the liquor in my glass.

"Why is mom sad?"

Shaking his head, my father mumbled, "Maybe me...too."

I slid my glass away before he could refill it as I questioned, "You're sad?"

Nodding his head, he slumped forward.

"She didn't die."

"Who?"

Without answering me, my father started to laugh.

Jumping up from the table, I ran to my mother's room. She was sitting on a chair next to her bed. I could tell she had been crying. I didn't have to ask her anything.

"Abigail." I slowly shook my head as she looked over at me with tears rolling down her cheeks. "She tried to kill herself."

Surprisingly, I wasn't sad, I was angry.

Running out of my mother's room and back into the kitchen, I stopped at the table.

Staring at my father, I shouted, "You're sad because she didn't die?"

He started to get up, then quickly slumped back down in the chair and smiled at me. Shaking my head at him, I felt sick. All sorts of things flashed through my mind before I dashed to my room, locked the door, and climbed out my window.

Only thinking of Hert now, I couldn't imagine what he was going through. First his father drinks himself to death, and now his mother is trying to kill herself. How could she do this to him? How could either of them do this to him? I stopped at Hert's window, his room was empty. Making my way around to the front of his house, I saw him walking in.

Knocking on his front door, I waited for him to answer. A minute passed and I knocked harder. Still, there was no answer. I opened the door and walked in. All the lights in the house were off, but I could see Hert sitting on the couch in the dark.

"Get out." He snapped at me, almost immediately.

Ignoring him, I walked over to where he was sitting.

"Is she okay?"

Hert gave me a stupid look, so I rephrased my question.

"Is she going to be okay?"

Shaking his head without looking directly at me, he growled, "Why are you here?"

"You shouldn't be by yourself," I insisted, stepping a little closer.

Jumping to his feet, Hert stood right in front of me.

"You don't know anything. I don't want you here, now leave."

Keeping my tone soft, I swore, "I'm not leaving."

Hert took a step back and glared at me for a moment.

"Okay, stay as long as you want."

Before I could say anything else, he turned and walked out the front door.

I stood there for a while before I decided his house was a little too creepy for me in the dark. Flipping the light switch up, I noticed nothing happened. With a sigh, I walked around flipping every switch, still nothing. Walking back to the couch, I sat down, and placed my head in my hands. What was I supposed to do? I couldn't let him stay here in this house like this. My father would never help, and Hert would not agree to hiding in my room, after what happened last time. Mr. Roberts told him he would help. Why wasn't he taking it? I knew that was a stupid question. Shaking my head at the situation, I decided to stay and wait for him to come back home.

Nudged awake, I realized I had fallen asleep. Hert sat down next to me on the couch. I scooted back a little, trying to think of everything I should say. As it turned out, when I looked at him, I knew there was nothing to say.

"Why are you still here?"

"Why wouldn't I be?"

There was a long pause before Hert relaxed his expression.

"You need to go home."

"Look, we don't have to talk, but I know you want me here...so...just stop."

"Its two a.m. We have school in the morning."

With a slight smirk, I informed, "Then, I guess, I'm riding with you tomorrow."

He scowled at me, warning, "That's a bad idea." As I rolled my eyes, he stressed, "I'm serious, Renni."

I didn't want to give him anything else to worry about.

"Fine. I'll go home."

Giving in with a pout, I felt I tried my best to be there for him.

Chapter 9

Mrs. Herterand was released after a few days. The psychiatric evaluation concluded that she had a breakdown. She was scheduled weekly appointments, and prescribed medication. Hert went to school every day, but nowhere else. I understood. Still, I missed seeing him outside of that. Especially, on my birthday, it was the first year I didn't go out to the pond, or see Hert. I had a nice dinner with the Roberts'. When I found out they were leaving to go to Spain for a week, I was instantly depressed. Then to my surprise, Mr. Roberts informed me that he had already spoken to my father, and if I wanted to, I could stay with Emerson at their house while they were away.

I stood in my room trying to decide what exactly to pack. It was Sunday night, and I was so excited, I was having a hard time concentrating. Not only did I get to stay with Emerson, I was going to be free from my house for a whole week. I didn't want to bring too much, but at the same time, seven days was a long time. I didn't want to have to come home early for any reason.

While laying my jeans and t-shirts out on my bed, my father walked in my room.

"Emerson's here."

"I'm almost ready." I lied.

He shook his head at my bag sitting empty on the floor, then turned and walked out. I grabbed my toothbrush and a few other items from my bathroom, knowing I should have done all this yesterday. When I stepped back into my room, Emerson was standing in my doorway.

"Sorry." I apologized, picking my bag up off the floor.

His smile was forgiving as he assured, "It's alright." He glanced around my room before asking, "Is that the shirt I gave you?"

Nodding, I smiled at the shirt pinned to my wall.

Just before Emerson's basketball season started he gave me a team shirt. I'm sure he was hoping I would wear it to his games, but since I felt the same way about school as I did living at home, I hung it on my wall.

"You know there is a game this Friday." Emerson reminded me while giving me a 'please wear it' look.

"Yes Em." Stuffing my clothes into my bag, I hoped he would leave it at that.

With a light sigh, he seemed to give up.

"Are you ready?"

Nodding at him, I zipped up my bag. I started to pick it up when Emerson gave me a 'don't even think about it' glare, and took my bag from me. Shaking my head with a slight laughed, I wondered if I would ever get used to him.

Emerson was definitely raised right. He was thoughtful and polite without thinking twice about it, like it was bred into him. He always did what he was told, and exactly what he was supposed to do. Full of compassion and understanding, he never raised his voice, or got angry. At this point, I knew, I would be devastated if I lost him.

We stopped in the kitchen, on our way out, to let my father know I was leaving. I wanted to make a face when he encouraged us to have a good time. Instead, I politely smiled so we could leave. Emerson gave a nod and polite smile also before opening the door for me as we left. He carefully placed my bag in his trunk and then we were on our way.

Half way to his house, a thought appeared in my mind that seemed worthy of questioning.

"So is your girlfriend mad that I'm staying with you?"

Smiling more to himself than at me, Emerson replied, "Would it matter to you if she was?"

"Not really, I was just curious."

"No, she just said as long as I understand once we get married…"

I couldn't let him finish before blurting, "You're getting married?"

"Not tomorrow or before we graduate. We have talked about it though."

Horrified at the thought, I questioned, "Why would you want to do that?"

"Why wouldn't I?"

Shaking my head at him, I fussed, "That's not an answer."

"Ren, most people plan on growing up and getting married. She loves me."

"She loves you, or the fact that you're Emerson Roberts?"

"That's not very nice." He scolded with a frown.
A sudden attack of guilt made me apologize.

"I'm sorry. I just think you have so much more to offer than your name."

"I love you, Ren, but you don't know her like I do."
Stunned, I couldn't believe what I heard come out of his mouth.

First of all, I did know her. Girls like Helena only cared about what was on the surface. That wasn't shocking to me and it made sense that Em couldn't tell the difference. What caught me by surprise was that he said he loved me. The rest of the way to his house, I couldn't say anything. No matter how hard I tried to, I came up empty. No one had ever said that they loved me. Not even as a thoughtless comment.

It was only eight o'clock when we arrived. I followed Emerson up to his room wondering what, if anything, I should say.

"The guest room is next door." He offered as he set my bag down on a chair in his room.
Staring at him, I nodded.

"Did you want to sleep in here?"
Shrugging, I actually did. I could see how that would be out of line. Still, that wasn't my issue.

With a heavy sigh, Em placed his arm around my shoulders. "I don't want to start the week off with you mad at me. This is supposed to be fun."

Looking up at him, I swore, "I'm not mad at you."

There was a thoughtful look in his eyes as he asked, "Then what's wrong?"

"You said you love me."

"I do. Don't you love me?"

I nodded, wrapping my arms around his sides and hugging him tight.

We sat on his bed in our pajamas, talking and laughing as it got later and later. The issue of where to sleep remained in the back of my mind. I was unsure of how to approach the subject. I didn't want it to come off as wanting to do more than just sleep. As it turned out, I didn't have to bring it up at all.

Emerson stretched out on his side of the bed.

"Are you staying in here?"

"Is that okay?"

He pulled the covers on the opposite side of the bed back with a soft smile. Mimicking his smile, I slid under them. I pulled the comforter around myself, and rolled onto my side with my back to him. Still on top of the comforter on his side of the bed, Emerson placed his arm over me.

Kissing the back of my head, he whispered, "Goodnight, I love you."

Nodding into my pillow, I assured, "Night, I love you, too."

Slowly closing my eyes, I felt more comfortable and relaxed than I had in my entire life as I drifted off to sleep.

Chapter 10

We stayed up late talking every night. My sleep was so peaceful I wasn't even tired in the mornings. Before I knew it, it was Friday. The Roberts were due back on Monday, leaving us with only the weekend before their return. It was so nice staying with Em. The best part was, at his house, we were in our own little world.

No matter how enjoyable staying with Emerson was, I was concerned that Hert had missed the last two days of school. Right after lunch Emerson dropped me off to go check on him. It turned out, Hert was sick. I was relieved that was all it was, and happy he didn't complain that much about me stopping by and staying awhile. After making him soup, and forcing him to take cold medicine, I left a glass of orange juice by his bed.

Opening the front door with a smile, I noticed an unhappy expression on Emerson's face as he looked me up and down.

"Why won't you wear the shirt I got you to wear on game nights?"

"Because I already told you, it was sweet of you to get it for me, but I'm never gonna wear it."

Almost pouting, he pressed, "But it has my number on the back."

"And that's why it's hanging on my wall," I chirped closing the door.

With a sigh he held my hand and walked me to his car.

"How is Hert?"

"Still a pain in the ass, but he should be good now. It took forever to get him to take medicine."

"You know, we are right by your house, we could stop and get your shirt." Emerson offered, reviving the whole game shirt discussion.

Making a face at him, I assured, "No thanks, I'm good."

He opened the passenger door for me and closed it behind me, once I slid in.

On the way to the game the car ride was fairly quiet. Assuming I had upset him, I agreed when he offered to let me wear his jacket. When we pulled up at the school, he parked the car, and handed me his keys.

"What are these for?"

"Helena went with her parents to visit family for the weekend. I thought you and I could go eat after the game. I brought a change of clothes. I'm going to shower before we go. You might want to wait in the car instead of hanging around outside the locker room."

"Sound's good."

Emerson seemed in a much better mood as we walked hand in hand into the gym. After giving him a good luck hug before he headed to the locker room, I found a place to sit in the stands, that wasn't too crowded and waited for the game to start.

Honestly, I didn't care for basketball. I went because it bothered me that no one ever came to watch Em play. Being a loyal friend, and Emerson's number one fan, I cheered every time he had the ball. It was one of the last games of the season and they won by two points. Happy for him, I left the bleachers to congratulate him. When I caught up to him, he hugged me. I told him to hurry so we could celebrate his seventh win before I headed out to the parking lot.

Almost at the exit door, I felt someone nudge me from behind.

"I think you left this."

When I turned around, I was caught off guard by a tall, blonde haired guy with an incredible smile.

"Huh?"

Laughing at me, he handed me a piece of paper.

"You left this."

Confused, I took the paper from him.

"I don't think this is mine."

Flashing his amazing smile at me again, he asked, "You're Ren, right?"

"Yea, but…"

He quickly cut me off, saying, "Then this is definitely yours."

Baffled, I opened the folded piece of paper as he walked away. It had the name Jackson and a phone number written on it. I quickly glanced up. When I did, he turned back, smiled, and winked at me. I couldn't help smiling in return.

Sitting in the passenger seat of Emerson's car, I waited for him to come out. While I waited, I smiled to myself thinking of Jackson's smile. I knew who he was. Jackson Thomas had quite a reputation with the girls at my school. I'd heard his name from time to time, but this was the first time I had actually seen him. There was no way I was going to call him. However, that smile of his seemed to stick in my mind. I was a bit smitten. The longer I dwelled on that smile, the happier it made me. By the time Emerson made it to the car, I was smiling uncontrollably.

Emerson drove us to a popular little place to eat. After we were seated and waited on, I looked up from our table and saw Jackson walk in with his arm around some girl. The second I saw him, I looked down at the table and smiled.

"What?"

Shaking my head, I continued to smile.

"I met Jackson earlier."

"I figured he would catch up to you sooner or later. He's been asking about you."

I felt a smile spread wide across my face as I questioned, "Really?"

"Do you like him?"

Trying to get a handle on my ridiculous smiling, I rolled my eyes.

"Please, I don't even know him."

Thankfully, our food arrived before I had to admit anything.

It just so happened, Jackson's table was two tables away from ours. The girl with him, was seated with her back to us. As I ate, I took the opportunity to sneak little peaks at Jackson, who was seated in full view. I could tell he was

71

full of himself. Every movement he made exuded confidence and rightfully so. He knew he was cute and it showed. I quickly found myself glancing over at him every few seconds, until our meal was over.

Emerson paid the check and we started to leave. As we walked toward the door, I glanced back one last time at Jackson. This time, he caught me. Smiling wide at me, he stood up from his table. I could feel my face turning red, knowing he was headed our way.

Jackson patted Emerson on the back, saying, "Hey, man. Practice tomorrow at your house."

"About one would be great," Emerson agreed.

"Then dinner at seven?" Jackson turned to me and asked.

"Are you seriously asking me out with your girl right there?" I questioned while pointing to his date.

His smile beamed as he informed, "I'm asking you right in front of your boy."

I watched Emerson smile while shaking his head at us.

"Emerson's not my boy, we're just friends."

"And she's not my girl, we're just on a date." He countered with a convincing smile.

I couldn't hold back my smile as I rolled my eyes and shook my head at him.

Jackson seemed to give up, but not before nudging me, quickly kissing me on the cheek and saying, "Maybe next time."

I stared at Emerson in disbelief as Jackson walked back to his date.

On the way back to Emerson's house, I couldn't stop thinking about Jackson. I mean really, what kind of guy gives me his number, instead of asking for mine? Asks me out, while he's already on a date? Then, has the nerve to kiss me?

"Are you thinking about Jackson?"

"Maybe a little," I admitted.

I could hear the smile in his voice as he questioned, "Are you going to go out with him?"

"I'm not sure that's a good idea. I mean, I've heard about him. He kinda has a reputation, ya know."

"Look at you, judging people before you get to know them." Emerson laughed.

I felt a little guilty at the truth in his accusation, even if he was just teasing me.

"So you're saying I should go out with him?"

"He's an alright guy. The only negative thing I think I should warn you about is that he has a one date rule."

"What's a one date rule?"

Slightly hesitant, he explained, "He only takes a girl out once."

"Why?"

"Because once is all it takes."

At first, I didn't understand, then as I watched his expression, I got it.

Back at Emerson's house, I put my pajamas on before stepping back into his room. I sat on his bed waiting for him while he took his turn changing in the bathroom. I couldn't help being disappointed. I only had one rule I held myself accountable to and it appeared as though, Jackson's one rule was the opposite of mine. As Emerson stepped out of the bathroom, I gave him a half-hearted smile. He climbed in bed and gave me a concerned look.

Sliding under the covers, I shared, "I won't be going out with Jackson."

"It will be his loss, not yours." He shared with a sweet smile.

Smiling back, I snuggled close before falling asleep.

Chapter 11

Barely opening my eyes, I rolled over and noticed Emerson wasn't in the room. I glanced at the clock and realized I slept late. Even though I decided it would be a bad idea to go out with Jackson, I still wanted to look cute when he arrived. I hopped out of bed and skipped to the bathroom. After brushing my teeth and washing my face, I stepped back into Em's room to find my bag. When I found it sitting on the chair by his dresser, I unzipped it, grabbed a hair thing, and my hairbrush.

I shouted, "I'm dressed," when there was a knock on the bedroom door.

Expecting Emerson, I was horrified when Jackson walked in instead.

Smiling wide, Jackson greeted, "Hey, you wanna come watch us practice?"

Standing there, with what I'm sure was a mortified expression, I blurted, "Okay," and rushed back to the bathroom.

I looked in the mirror, and sighed. Why couldn't I have at least brushed my hair before seeing him again?

After I was dressed and presentable, I headed downstairs. Walking through the kitchen, I declined breakfast from the Roberts' housekeeper Fidora, and stepped outside. I could hear Jackson and Emerson talking as I made my way around the garage.

Deciding to eavesdrop a little, I heard Emerson first.

"She didn't say anything to me."

"I can't believe she didn't say yes." Jackson laughed.

Curious to find out if they were talking about me, I continued listening.

Emerson's tone was serious as he replied, "She's different. You can't charm her into anything."

"She likes me." Jackson insisted.

"Whatever you say." Emerson laughed.

"If I were you, I wouldn't have gotten outta bed this morning. She's so damn cute."

Wanting to embarrass Jackson for that little bed comment, I walked around the corner asking, "Who's so damn cute?"

Without skipping a beat, Jackson smiled wide and winked. "You."

My eyes were wide and I could feel my face turning red as I walked to the side of the court and sat down.

I watched them practice for about an hour before they took a break. The three of us walked inside to have lunch. Fidora was giving me a strange smile, tilting her head towards Jackson as she handed me my plate.

"What do you like to do? When you're not hanging out with Roberts, that is." Jackson questioned before I could take a bite of my lunch.

I tried to think quickly. Realizing I really didn't do anything else aside from visiting Hert and making my father mad, I shrugged my shoulders.

"Just regular stuff."

"Okay..."

That was the third time, today, I was tongue tied around him.

Quietly taking a bite of my sandwich, I decided to make it my personal mission for the day to get the best of him.

Raising and eyebrow, I asked, "So, what do you like to do? Aside from what you're known for that is."

Emerson almost choked on his water. "I'm going to go take a shower." Shaking his head at me, he got up from the table.

Jackson smiled wide before questioning, "And what is it that I'm known for?"

Mentally shouting 'damn it,' I smirked at him.

"Your dates are sorta infamous."

"Well, outside of dating, there's basketball."

"That's all?" I questioned, hoping there a little more to him than sports and sex.

"I have an academic scholarship for college."

"I thought you were a junior?"

"I'm in the honors program."

Tilting my head to the side, I was genuinely surprised. "I didn't know that."

While Jackson appeared uncomfortable, I was intrigued.

There were only about fifteen students at my school enrolled in the honors program. These select students, not only ranked highest in our school, they were amongst the highest in the state. Their classes were in an entirely different building from everyone else's and their day was divided between our school and the local college.

"How did you get in?"

Relaxing a bit, he explained, "I was picked after one of my teachers suggested I take the test."

"Huh, I didn't know you were so smart." I thought out loud.

"I'm just good at tests because it's easy for me to memorize stuff."

"Do you have a photographic memory or something like that?"

"It's actually called an eidetic memory, because it's not just things I see. There's a bunch of big words that explain it, but to be honest it's not a big deal." He corrected with a shrug.

"It's a big deal." I assured, unintentionally flirting with him.

Leaning closer, he asked, "What are you good at?"
The only thing that came to mind was getting in trouble.

With a laugh, I sat up tall, sharing, "I'm good at everything I do."

"What do you like to do?"

"Whatever I want." I replied, wishing he would stop asking me that.

"Do you want to go out with me?"
I wanted to say yes. What I didn't want was to appear as eager as I was. Deciding to make him work for it, I rolled my eyes, and stood up. Thankfully, Emerson walked back into the kitchen, giving me time to put him off a little longer. At this point, I was definitely going to say yes.

When Emerson sat down, he swayed the conversation toward basketball. I enjoyed listening to them talk about their team. It was very cute, the way Jackson seemed to get all excited about their wins and points scored. And, I found out another interesting fact. Jackson had been on the varsity team since freshman year. Then, out of nowhere, Hert popped into my head. I thought of what he would say about me going out with Jackson, and I started to second guess myself.

Jackson stood up, breaking my concentration.

"Oh, I have to go."

"Got a hot date?" I blurted without thinking.

"That depends, will you go out with me?"

Shaking my head, I watched him sigh, and make a pouty face.

Emerson politely stated, "Tell your parents, I said thank you for letting you come practice today."

Jackson laughed, "Yea, my dad said he didn't think we needed the practice, but we should get that number four over here 'cause he needs it."

Emerson nodded, laughing back.

"So you have plans with your parents tonight?" I questioned, wondering why he asked me out last night for tonight.

"Nah, I have to help my dad clean the garage." He patted Em on the back, saying, "See ya later man."

A little disappointed to see him go, I chirped, "Bye," with a little smile.

"Later Ren," He replied with a wink.

I couldn't help smiling wide.

Emerson and I watched a few movies in the living room before deciding to call it a night. Even though it seemed boring for a Saturday evening, lying in his room talking had become my favorite thing to do. I figured it was in my best interest that I didn't say yes before Jackson left, but I was a little disappointed too. Until, he called. Feeling a little silly at how excited I was, it was my first call from a boy. When he asked me out again, this time, I said yes. I could hear the smile in his voice as he said goodbye. Thrilled, against my better judgment, I was going to go out on my first date, and with Jackson Thomas of all people.

Chapter 12

Even though my father was out of town, I felt it was best if Jackson did not pick me up from my house. There were no clear rules for dating, but my father had made it clear, multiple times, that leaving the house with anyone other than Emerson was frowned upon. The Roberts returned from house hunting in Spain and Mrs. Roberts agreed to allow Jackson to pick me up from their house. Since our date was at seven, Em was picking me up at five. My mother was gone for the day, so I walked over to Hert's to kill some time before I had to get ready.

Hert appeared surprised to see me when he opened the door.

"How ya doin'," I asked as I walked in.

"You're in a good mood."

"I have a date, tonight."

He raised his eyebrows in curiosity. "With…?"

"Jackson Thomas." I replied with a wide smile.

His expression was less than excited as he walked to his room and I followed.

Over the last week, Jackson had hollered my name across the parking lot, the hallway, and even the cafeteria at school. Smiling wide at me each time he caught my attention, I would roll my eyes and shake my head with a smile in return. Each time, Hert gave me a disapproving glare and I just shrugged him off.

Why did he always have to be like this? I wished he could be happy for me. I knew what he was thinking, and I knew what everyone said about Jackson. That aside, just because every other girl he went out with slept with him, didn't mean I was going to. I will admit, there was a certain amount of carnal curiosity associated with going on a date with him. What would a date with the infamous Jackson Thomas be like? Would I be tempted to sacrifice my one rule for his? What was it about him that made all those girls give in so easily? Still, Hert should know better than to think I would.

Refusing to let him spoil my good mood, I flopped down on his bed.

"Ya know, this is my first real date, you don't have to be a jerk about it."

"As long as you know, he only takes a girl out once."

Narrowing my eyes at him, I goaded, "At least he wants to take me out first," as he sat down on the corner of his bed.

"So that's why you said yes? You wanna have sex?"
My reference to Carmella and his relationship must have stung him.

"If I do, you have no right to say a word about it. You're doing it."
His expression instantly changed.

"If you do, it should be with someone who really cares about you, not some guy who's just trying to get into your pants."
I couldn't help feeling a tad shocked by his concern.

"I'm not going to sleep with him, but I like him and you know what, I think he likes me too."

Hert nodded. "It's just that..." Before he got too sentimental with me, I stopped him. "I know you're just lookin' out for me. I'm seventeen now, Hert. I think that makes me old enough for whatever I decide to do."
Slightly smiling at me, he dropped the subject.

After a while, I walked back home to get ready for Emerson to pick me up so Jackson could take me out on our date. Flipping through the clothes in my closet, I settled on a strappy turquoise dress that was fitted at the top and flowed down almost brushing the floor, easily dressed down with sandals and a thin sweater, left open of course. Not to sound too conceited, but I looked damn good. Pleased with myself, I figured, if one date was really all he wanted, he would regret it for the rest of his life. I carefully applied my makeup, making sure it was perfect. In lieu of spending too much time on my hair, I pulled it into a loose up-do.

Emerson arrived to pick me up. He stayed long enough for me to leave a note for my mother. Then, we were on our way back to his house.

"You look very nice," Em complimented, glancing over at me.

"Thanks."

"Are you excited?"

"I am a little nervous too."

"Why?"

Feeling a twinge of embarrassment, I shared, "I've never been on an actual date before."

With a sweet smile he assured, "He's the one that should be nervous. Not only do you look incredible, you're pretty intimidating."

Laughing at the thought of anyone finding me intimidating, I reached over and held his hand the rest of the way.

We made it to Emerson's house about thirty minutes before Jackson arrived. While Emerson and I waited in the kitchen, because Mrs. Roberts said I should make an entrance when Jackson came to pick me up, I started to feel my stomach knotting up. I liked Jackson. He made me smile every time I saw him, and as much as I hated to admit it, I really wanted there to be more than one date and more than one reason why he was taking me out.

Finally, I heard a knock on the front door. Looking up at Emerson, I took a deep breath and smiled.

Mrs. Roberts alerted, "Rennillia, Jackson is here."

When I stepped into the living room, I saw Jackson standing next to Mr. Roberts.

Jackson smiled wide, the second I caught his eye. "Hey!"

Walking towards him, I smiled back. "Hi."

Mrs. Roberts and Emerson left the room, while Mr. Roberts remained standing between Jackson and I.

Mr. Roberts focused his attention on Jackson. "I realize I am not Rennillia's father, however, you are picking her up from my care. I expect you to treat her with respect and return her to her home no later than twelve. Do we understand each other, Jackson?"

"Yes sir." Jackson replied with a serious expression.
Mr. Roberts walked past me and smiled as he headed to the kitchen.

"Have a nice time."
Although, I was still nervous, I could feel excitement building inside of me. This was it. I was really going on a date with him.

Taking turns smiling at each other, it took us a little while to actually leave. Jackson opened the front door for me. He placed his arm around my shoulders as we walked out to his truck.

"I like your truck," I shared, trying to break the nervous silence.

Jackson leaned close before he opened the door for me. "I like you."
I couldn't help smiling as I climbed in.

"Where would you like to go?" He asked as we pulled away from the Roberts' house.

"Wherever you wanna take me."
Jackson looked over at me with a wide smile, and winked.

"I think we should go to dinner first."
Did he really just say that?' I quickly answered myself, 'yes he did'. I wasn't quite use to him, but that was how Jackson was. Often inappropriate, his funny and cheerful disposition made up for it.

It was a complete and total surprise when we pulled up to the valet at Mansurs'.

"This place okay?"

"Umm… Sure."
The valet opened the door for me, and I watched Jackson grab his suit jacket and a tie from behind the seat. Quickly putting them on, he walked over to me. Thinking 'well aren't you full of surprises', I wished I had worn heels. Doing the next best thing, I slipped off my little sweater even though it was chilly out.

As we walked to the restaurant door, Jackson leaned to my ear and whispered, "Damn, are you trying to kill me?"
Rolling my eyes, I shook my head at him, and smiled.

Apparently Jackson's question of what to do was simply out of courtesy. Clearly, he had the evening already planned out; since it turned out he made reservations at Mansurs'.

We were quickly seated at a little table for two in the corner. I started to take my seat across the table from him, when he pulled my chair right next to his and motioned for me to sit. We were so close together, it was hard to keep from brushing against him. Looking down at my menu, I didn't realize I was wiggling my fingers against it.

"Are you nervous?"

Keeping my eyes fixed on the menu, I admitted, "A little."

I could hear the smile in his voice as he questioned, "Why?"

"I haven't ever been on a real date before."

Jackson was silent for a moment. I felt him kiss my shoulder. Turning to look at him, I realized we were face to face. Leaning in, he softly kissed my lips. I was speechless.

"Don't be nervous." Jackson whispered as he slowly pulled away.

It took a moment of me staring at him to realize he was right. With the most anticipated event of the evening out of the way, I relaxed.

Jackson wrapped his arm around my shoulders as we left the restaurant. In his truck, I slid to the middle, sitting right next to him. With his arm back around my shoulders, I tucked my legs under my dress and leaned against him. Even if I had been on a thousand dates before, I was sure this one would have been the best.

"It's only nine. What do ya want to do now?"

"Well, you're doing pretty good so far. You pick."

"Do you wanna get a drink?" He questioned with a wide smile.

"Like a drink, drink?"

"My cousin Gus owns The Bar. We can't go in the front, but we can have a beer in the back…that is, if you want."

Pretending to think it over, I waited a minute before answering. "Okay."

He made a u-turn, and we were headed to The Bar.

Pulling around back when we arrived, we got out and walked to the back door. Inside, Jackson opened the door to a small room. He asked me to wait for him before sharing that he would be back in just a few minutes. While I waited, I looked around the room and spotted a small bed against the wall. I felt a pang of Hert's impending 'I told you so'. Standing there waiting, I decided to give him the benefit of the doubt, seeing as he had been incredibly respectful so far.

It wasn't long before I heard voices outside the door, making their way to the room.

I saw Jackson first, then a stocky, red haired man with a full beard, holding two beers. "Ren this is my cousin Gus."
I smiled with a slight nod as Gus handed Jackson and me our drinks.

Gus smiled. "Nice to meet ya."
As he left the room, Gus motioned for Jackson to follow him.

Even though Jackson closed the door behind them, I heard Gus. "What the hell is the matter with you boy, bringin' that dago girl to my bar? Does her father know she's out with you?"

There was a long pause before I heard Jackson. "No, but..." Before he could fully reply, Gus cut him off, insisting, "There is somethin' really wrong with you boy."
Then, there was silence.

The door slowly opened and Jackson walked in.

"I don't want you to get in trouble by bringing me here."

"It's all good, Gus just gets sensitive now and then."

Out of curiosity, I questioned, "So does he get all upset every time you bring a girl here, or is it just the dago ones?"

He appeared a bit surprised. "I've never brought a girl here before." Tilting my head, I raised an eyebrow, silently questioning him as he assured, "I really haven't."

"And the bed?"

"Gus stays here when he gets in trouble with his wife."
I believed what he was saying. However, I wasn't entirely sure if it was because he was telling the truth, or that I wanted it to be true.

Jackson took off his jacket and laid it at the head of the bed before he sat down on the bed and patted the spot next to him. I took a sip of my beer and sat down. I shivered a little and realized I left my sweater in his truck.

"Are you cold?"

Nodding, I took another sip. "I left my sweater in your truck."

Jackson scooted closer, and placed his arm around me.

"Are you having a good time so far?"

Holding back a smile, I nodded.

"Are you?"

"Yea, I am." He replied as if he was unsure at one point that he would be.

Happy with his response, I chirped, "Good."

We smiled back and forth at each other a few times before he took my beer, and set it on a small table next to his. He tugged me closer and smiled. This time, I was ready when he leaned in and kissed me.

Our second kiss was better than the first.

Jackson pulled back, smiled, and kissed me a third time. With one of his hands around my waist and the other resting on my arm, our kiss continued. Before I knew it, his hand was in my hair, loosening my up-do, and his lips were trailing down my neck. Seeing as I had only been kissed a few times in my life, and never officially made out with anyone, I thought this was acceptable behavior for a date. When his lips reached the top of my shoulder, Jackson pulled back with another smile and returned his kisses to my lips. Caught up in the moment, I wrapped my arms around his neck, and pressed myself against him.

When I felt his hand moving up my thigh, I quickly pulled back. Jackson moved his hand after my discouraging look, and started to kiss me, again. Until, his hand ran across the top of my dress, around to the back and started to unzip it.

"Jackson," I snapped, grabbing hold of his arm.

He appeared a bit baffled as he questioned, "What's wrong?"

"I don't…"

"That's okay, I have something."

My heart instantly sank as I pushed away from him, and stood up.

"Did you want the light off?"

"No. What the hell do you think is gonna happen here?"

Jackson appeared apologetic. "I just thought…"

"Oh, I know what you thought."

"Why are you so mad?"

"Seriously? I'm not just some girl that you only take out once."

Nodding, he agreed, "I know you're not."

"Then what the hell made you think I would sleep with you?"

"The way you were kissing me…"

I glared at him, knowing that wasn't why.

With a shrug, he confessed. "You spend the night with Roberts when his parents are gone, and I've heard about you and Scott."

I started to feel sick. How was I so stupid? Hert was right, and I was wrong.

Disappointed, yet prideful, I firmly stated, "Take me home."

Standing up, he reached out to hold my hand. Denying him, I crossed my arms in front of my chest.

"I don't wanna take you home."

"I don't care what you want, and for your information, ass, I've never done 'it' with Hert, Emerson or anyone else for that matter."

Jackson stared at me for a moment.

"But, I really like you."

"Yea, I liked you too, now take me home or I'll call Hert to come and get me."

Nodding, he agreed, "I'll take you home."

We left The Bar and he drove me straight home.

When we pulled up outside my house, I started to get out and noticed Jackson was getting out too. With a heavy sigh, I slammed his door and quickly walked to my house.

"Oh, I know you don't think you're getting a goodnight kiss," I assured as he followed.

"Ren, wait."

Turning to face him, I snapped, "What?"

"Can I take you out tomorrow?"

Stunned, I didn't know what to say.

"Let me take you out again," he coaxed with a genuine smile.

Caught off guard, I softened my tone. "I can't. I have plans. Hert and I are going to Emerson's."

"Can I meet you over there?"

"I guess, if you want."

Smiling wide, he knew he had been forgiven.

"Seems like a waste, you have a whole hour until you had to be home."

I shook my head, rolled my eyes, and smiled. "Goodnight, Jackson."

Smiling his smile, he winked at me then headed back to his truck.

Inside my house, I walked to my room. Maybe Jackson did like me after all. I guess, I couldn't blame him for trying, and it's possible that if I had slept with someone before I would've wanted to also. Starting to get excited about seeing him again, I opened my door smiling.

"What the hell?" I blurted, when I saw Hert sitting on my bed.

He hadn't come near my house since we got in trouble with my father for washing dishes.

"I came to see how your date went, but I see it went pretty well," he snapped.

Confused, I stared at him before I glanced in the mirror and realized all my lipstick was off and my hair was down and wild.

"It did go very well, and by the way, I didn't put out, if that's what you're sayin'."

I could see the relief on his face as he pretended not to care.

"It's none of my business."

"Oh, and I got asked out on a second date."

Giving him a 'so there' look, I grabbed my pajamas, and headed into the bathroom.

I was a little surprised to see Hert still on my bed when I came out.

"Are you sleeping over?"

Without a second thought, he replied, "Nope," and climbed out my window.

I closed my window and hopped into bed, deciding, Hert could be nice when he wanted to, and my date with Jackson was still the best first date ever.

Chapter 13

I woke up with butterflies in my stomach. I couldn't wait to see Jackson, again. Hert kept glancing at me with a suspicious expression as he drove us to Emerson's, in his mother's car. As sure as I was that Jackson meant it when he said he really liked me, I was still surprised when we pulled up to Emerson's and his truck was parked outside. I was ecstatic, but smart enough to know I shouldn't let it show. Walking up the back driveway, we saw Emerson and Jackson out on the court. Trying hard not to smile at the sight of him, I stood up tall, doing my best to pretend I wasn't thrilled to see him. The moment Jackson saw me he stopped playing, and made his way over to us. Hert gave me an 'I don't like him' grunt, while I gave him a dirty 'knock it off' look in return. When Jackson caught up to us Hert turned and walk over to Emerson, making it clear Jackson wasn't worth his time.

Shrugging Hert and his attitude off, Jackson stepped right in front of me.

"I'm glad you showed up," he shared with a smile.

"You knew I was coming over here."

His smile spread as he asked, "Then are you glad I showed up?"

Unable to fight a smile of my own, I rolled my eyes at him. Incredibly pleased with my response, he quickly kissed my cheek before jogging back to the court.

Hert's unhappy expression was all too clear as he walked back to my side. I stood at the edge of the court, watching them practice while Hert stayed next to me giving Jackson 'I hope you trip and fall' looks every chance he got. Nudging Hert, I gave him a disapproving stare before I walked into the house to tell the Roberts' hello. Fidora was in the kitchen preparing lunch, and after telling her 'hi', I stepped into the living room and found Mrs. Roberts coming down the stairs.

"Rennillia, how are you today, dear? I'll be back this evening," she quickly stated before continuing down the stairs, and out the front door.

I guess even Mrs. Roberts, who was all about appearance and making the proper entrance, ran late every once and awhile. With nothing to do inside, I walked back through the kitchen, and after Fidora notified me that lunch was ready, I walked out the back door.

The three of them were standing together. A little surprised at first, I quickly realized Hert was threatening Jackson. I dashed over knowing there was fixing to be a fight by Hert's serious expression and Jackson's smirk.

Scooting right in the middle, I smiled, informing, "Lunch is ready."

Emerson, who had obviously been trying to be the peacemaker, urged, "Let's go eat,"

Hert gave Jackson a hard glare before turning and walking into the house. Emerson shook his head and sighed as he followed.

We both stood there for a minute, staring in the direction Hert and Emerson went.

"Are you gonna come eat?"

"I think your friend might need a minute."

"Yea, he doesn't like you very much."

"Good thing I'm not tryin' to get with him then, huh?" he laughed.

Slightly offended, I questioned, "'Cause you're trying to 'get with' me?"

"Trying, not succeeding."

How could I not like him, when he made me smile just by being himself?

Rolling my eyes, I admitted, "You're actually not doing too bad."

Smiling wide, he wrapped his arms around me. Unsure if it was his kiss or the air that gave me a chill, I shivered slightly as goose bumps covered my arms.

"Guess I am doing pretty good." Jackson all but cheered with an air of pride about him.

Rolling my eyes with a smile, I laughed, "Don't get all excited, I'm just cold."

Making a pouty face, he let go, and walked over to the garage. Swiftly making his way back, carrying a green hoodie, he handed it to me. He helped me put it on, zipped it all the way up then kissed me, again.

"Just checkin'." He shared with a smile, when I gave him a startled look.

That was the moment I knew, I was completely smitten with him.

Emerson and Hert were still inside, while Jackson and I sat outside on the court. Holding one of my hands Jackson tugged on the bottom of the opposite sleeve of his hoodie that I was wearing.

"Please let me take you out again?"

With a light sigh, I shook my head. "I don't think so."

He appeared slightly disappointed, but still cheerful.

"Why not?"

"I don't like the idea of you taking me where you've taken other girls."

"I haven't."

"You can't take me to that restaurant every time, it's really expensive, and I don't wanna go to little rooms with beds in them either."

"Then I know the perfect place. All you have to do is say yes."

Exhaling loudly, I agreed, "Okay."

Smiling wide, he tugged on my sleeve then kissed me until we heard footsteps close behind.

Looking up, I was a little embarrassed to see Hert and Emerson standing there. Knowing my face was turning red, I leaned my head into Jackson's shoulder. I heard Hert mumble something before Emerson walked around us.

"Sorry to interrupt you two."

Hert snapped, "Let's go."

I could feel myself frowning as I started to say, "But I'm not…"

Jackson spoke up, "I'll take Ren home."

"No you won't." Hert stated with an irritated expression.

Pulling away from me, Jackson stood up.

91

"Excuse me?"

Jumping up, I looked at Hert and ordered, "Just go to the car, I'll be there in a second."

Hert turned and walked away, after giving Jackson a hateful glare.

"What's his problem?" Jackson fussed, stepping closer to me.

Shaking my head with a sigh, I explained, "He's just kinda that way. He doesn't know you."

Pulling me close, Jackson lightly kissed me.

"Do you have to go?"

Nodding, I gave him a soft smile. "Yea, I better."

"Can I pick you up for school tomorrow?"

"I'm not allowed to ride with anyone but Emerson."

"Then can you get to school early tomorrow so I can see you before class?"

"If it's okay with Em, I will."

"Sure." Emerson confirmed as Jackson looked over at him.

I smiled at Emerson before turning back to Jackson and blurting, "Oh, your jacket."

I started to give Jackson his hoodie back when he stopped me.

"I'll get it from you in the morning."

Smiling, I zipped it back up. He kissed me one more time before he hesitantly let go. I gave Emerson a smile and little wave then headed to the car.

The closer I got to the car, the more irritated I became. Watching Hert's unpleasant expression as he refused to look at me, I got in, and slammed the door. With a slight grunt he pulled out of the Roberts' back driveway.

About five minutes into our drive, I couldn't keep quiet.

"I cannot believe you."

"Me? I can't believe you would do that in front of everybody."

Furious, I argued, "What? Kiss him? And what everybody? We were outside by ourselves, until you so rudely interrupted us."

Pulling off to the side of the road, Hert stopped the car and turned to me.

"Kissed? He was all over you!"

Taking a moment to reflect, I shouted, "No, he wasn't!"

"Guys like Jackson only take a girl out for one reason."

Narrowing my eyes, I reminded him, "Oh, as opposed to guys that sneak over to a girl's house when her parents aren't home for one thing, and don't even bother to take her out."

"Why do you always have to bring her up?"

"Because, I know what you do, and you don't know him."

"Neither do you."

"Both you and Emerson said he only takes a girl out once. He asked me out again, that night, after he took me home. I know he has a reputation, Hert, but in case you didn't realize it, so do you and I."

"That's different."

"Whether it's true or not, everybody here gets talked about, and I don't care what people say. I'm going to keep seeing him, because I like him. Just like I'm friends with you, because I like you, and if it just so happens he gets that one thing from me, that is between me and him. It has nothing to do with you."

Without another word, Hert pulled the car back onto the road, and continued to my house.

Stopping in front of my house, Hert and I looked at each other. My father's car was sitting in the driveway, which meant he was home.

"Do you want me to run you back to Roberts' house, and have him bring you home?"

Shaking my head, I declined. "I'm already here."

Hert appeared worried as he questioned, "Are you sure?"

I got out of the car, and walked to my front door. I wasn't worried about my father finding out Hert gave me a ride home, because he never watched for me to get in. However, I was still disappointed he was back.

Slowly walking inside, I unsuccessfully tried to go straight to my room.

"Where have you been?" my father questioned as I took Jackson's hoodie off, and tossed it on the couch.

Making my way back to the kitchen, I replied, "Emerson's."

My father narrowed his eyes at me.

"How was your date?"

I swallowed hard. "Sorry?"

"Don't play dumb with me, it's all over town!"

Standing there staring at him, I felt sick.

"Did I give you permission?" He questioned through gritted teeth.

"No, sir."

He stood up, hollering, "Do you think you can just do whatever you want?"

Thinking 'yes', I answered, "No, sir."

"Yes you do. It's bad enough you disobey me, but to disrespect me with that taig."

I must have made a face at him, because I was promptly slapped right across it.

Turning to walk away, I mumbled, "Does taig mean not Emerson?"

My father jerked me back by my arm, causing me to hit the table. It scooted a few inches across the floor as the pain in my hip caused me to lose my balance.

Catching me by my face, he leaned down eye to eye with me. "It means stay your ass away from that mick."

As he let go, I sat on the floor.

I watched him start to walk off. It was one thing for my father to hate Hert as a person, but how could he dislike Jackson simply because he was Irish.

Scrambling to my feet, I shouted, "Why?"

In a fury, he turned around.

"Are you questioning me?"

"Yes."

With a stunned expression, he shouted, "What?"

As sarcastic as I could, I spouted, "Yes, sir."

That was all it took for the back of my father's hand to go right across my eye.

"What the hell's wrong with you?" I snapped, holding my fingers against the outside corner of my eye.

Unsure of why that came out of my mouth, I was just as shocked as he was.

Grabbing the front of my shirt, my father spit in my face, and snarled, "Mignotta, merdoso."

Everything else was pretty much a blur after that.

It seemed as though it was never going to end, and I couldn't take it anymore.

"I'm sorry... I'm sorry." Crying, I lied, "I... I was trying to...to make him jealous... Emerson has a girlfriend... I'm sorry..."

My father instantly stopped. He stared at me in disgust before he turned and walked away. Curling up on the kitchen floor, I wanted to throw up. I made myself sick. How could I have said I was sorry?

It took me awhile, but I finally got up, and grabbed Jackson's hoodie as I made my way to my room. Not only had I cried like a baby, I pretended I was using Jackson.

Luckily, the only real mark on my face was a tiny cut on the corner of my eye, where my father's ring caught me. I knew the red blotches across my face would go away, since they weren't already turning into bruises. That would make it much easier to explain my eye. The rest of me was nothing that long sleeves couldn't remedy. I took a shower, and other than my hip, I wasn't all that sore.

Slowly getting into bed, I started to close my eyes. There was a light tap on my window. Lying there, I debated on whether or not to open it. Knowing Hert would be worried if I didn't acknowledge him, I sat up, and motioned for him to come in.

"Go lock my door," I whispered as he climbed in.

He did as he was told before sitting down on the little bench by my bed.

I pulled my comforter up to my chin, asking, "Is everything okay?"

"You tell me."

"My father doesn't know you dropped me off," I shared, waiting for him to relax.

"Then why?" he questioned, pulling my comforter down.

"Apparently, you're not the only one that doesn't like Jackson. He said it's all over town that I went out with him."

"Are you hurt?" he whispered, looking at my arms, shoulder, and then to my eye.

"Just my pride."

Hert gave me a strange look.

"I said, I was sorry."

Exhaling loudly, he closed his eyes, and shook his head.

"Are you gonna stay?" I asked, hoping he would.

He appeared as though he wished he could. "I can't."

"Okay, see you tomorrow," I said, forcing a smile.

Hert nodded, and climbed out of my window.

Curling up in my comforter, I rolled onto my side. I hoped Jackson would be okay with just hanging out at Emerson's. I still wanted to see him, but I wasn't sure he was worth getting my ass kicked to do it. I really did like him. More than any other guy, I had ever liked.

Chapter 14

Excited and a little nervous when Emerson and I pulled into the parking lot at school, Jackson was already there. Em looked over at me as I looked at him, smiling wide. Shaking his head with a slight laugh, he let go of my hand. As the car came to a stop, I watched Jackson walk up, and open my door. I smiled at him before I grabbed my books, and his hoodie from the back seat. Hopping out, I handed Jackson his hoodie. Flashing his incredible smile at me, he took my books. He set them in the bed of his truck before putting his hoodie on, and wrapping his arms around me.

Jackson leaned against his truck, holding me against him. Glancing around to make sure no one was looking first, he quickly kissed me.

"I'm going to go find Helena, see you two later," Emerson shared as he walked past us.

When we both turned our heads to say goodbye, Jackson asked, "What happened to your eye?"
I didn't think about anyone being that close to my face.

I fluffed it off, saying, "Oh, it's just a little cut."

"Does it hurt?"
I shook my head.

"Has anyone kissed it?"
I gave him a strange look before he softly kissed the corner of my eye. I really wanted to kiss him back but since we were at school I couldn't.

"Thank you," I whispered.

Jackson frowned slightly. "Your friend is here."
Turning around, I saw Hert walking up to us.

Even though I turned my back to Jackson, he didn't let go of me. Adjusting himself lower, against his truck, he rested his chin on my shoulder with his arms snug around my ribs.

"You alright?" he asked, completely ignoring Jackson.

"Yea," I replied as Hert walked past us.

Jackson kissed my cheek, and asked, "Why wouldn't you be alright?"

"Maybe, 'cause some guy has his hands all over me in the parking lot," I fibbed.

I could feel his smile on my cheek. "Lucky guy, I wouldn't mind having my hands all over you."

"Jackson," I blurted, turned to face him, and popped him on the arm.

Pulling me close, he asked, "What are you doing after school?"

"I might go to Emerson's," I answered, hoping he wanted to go there too.

With a light smile, he offered, "Since you said you would go out with me again, how about tonight?"

"It's a school night."

He looked around, then quickly kissed me.

"That's why I'm taking you to my house."

"Your house?"

"My parents will be there."

Not only was I the exception to his one date rule, now he was taking me to see his parents?

I didn't know what to say, but an involuntary, "Okay," slipped out through a smile.

To hell with my father.

Wrapping his arms around my neck, Jackson tucked his face between one of his arms, and started kissing down my neck. Assuming he was trying to hide this very inappropriate display of affection with the sleeves of his hoodie, I leaned my head against his shoulder. I assumed it looked like we were hugging. He pulled away slowly at first then quickly let go.

"What the... What happened?"

Confused, I took a step back.

"What?"

Appearing as though I had hurt his feelings, Jackson suggested, "We still have about fifteen minutes, let's sit in my truck."

I didn't understand what was wrong, until we were inside the cab. He pulled the top of my sweater to the side, revealing that it was covering a thin tank top.

"Was it that jackass?"

I thought, 'yes, my father is a jackass' as I questioned, "Who are you talking about?"

"Is that why he asked if you were alright?"

With a heavy sigh, I replied, "No."

"Then what the hell happened to you?" he demanded. Feeling uneasy about the situation, I scooted back.

The look on his face was hard to explain. It was somewhere between hurt and pity. Scowling at him, I crossed my arms in front of my chest. I searched my mind for something to say without directly lying to him. The more I thought about what to say, the more offended I became. Who the hell did he think he was? I had known him for about ten minutes, and he was already questioning me. So what if he took me out, and so what if I let him kiss me. That gave him no right to demand I tell him anything.

I narrowed my eyes at him.

"Nothing."

Reaching his hand out to me, Jackson asked, "Is that why he asked if you were okay?"

Shrugging his hand away, I stated, "Hert didn't do anything to me."

He shook his head, rephrasing, "He asked if you were okay because he knew you were hurt?"

Clinching my teeth, I nodded.

"Do you need to go home?"

"No."

"Did you fall or something?"

I recalled losing my balance after hitting the table.

"I guess, something like that,"

With a light sigh Jackson leaned his head toward me. "I can take you to my house some other time."

And there it was.

As Jackson continued his sympathetic gaze, I sat up tall. Hert and I understood each other when it came to these matters. In fact, when we were kids we used to compare bruises, and of course, Hert always came out ahead. Emerson, although he probably had never been in trouble a day in his life, was understanding and never pushed for an explanation. That was just his way.

There was no way Jackson would or could understand. No normal guy wants a damaged girl.

"You don't have to be nice about it. I understand."

Confusion spread across his face as he asked, "What am I being nice about?"

"If you don't want to…"

"Do you have anything important in your classes today?"

I shook my head at him. "No. Why?"

"You wanna skip?"

"You're gonna skip?"

"No, you are. I mean, if you want to. I don't have classes today."

"Then why are you here?"

Smiling wide, Jackson informed, "So I can see you."

I had to bite my bottom lip to keep from smiling wide.

"Is that a yes?"

With a soft smile, I nodded.

When Jackson left to tell Emerson we were leaving, I assumed Em would tell Hert. After a brief thought of, 'I am going to get in so much trouble for this', I wondered where we would go. It was crazy how happy Jackson made me. His smile was so infectious, it was nearly impossible for me not to be happy around him.

Glancing out of his truck window, I watched him jog back to the truck.

"You ready?"

I scooted right next to him. Jackson quickly kissed my cheek after starting up his truck. Placing his arm around me, he pulled out of the school parking lot.

"Still up for wherever I wanna take you?"

"That depends on what you plan to do when we get there."

"Whatever you let me," he assured with a smile.

Shaking my head as I rolled my eyes at him, I wondered where he was taking me.

When we came upon a little wooded area, Jackson drove his truck between some trees, and pulled around to a small clearing. Leaning back, I gave him a suspicious look.

He stopped the truck, and pulled the keys out of the ignition. "No, this isn't a place I take girls to."

"Really?"

"My house isn't far from here. My cousins and I used to wander around back here when we were kids."

"So why are we here?"

Leaning in, he placed a soft kiss against my lips.

"I don't know where else to take you, you're supposed to be at school."

I took a deep breath as I nodded.

The anxious feeling of being alone with him was instantly replaced by aggravation when his expression turned serious.

"Look, I'm just gonna say it. If you fell or had an accident, okay, but if someone did that to you... Ren, that's not okay."

"Is that why you brought me out here? So you can question me some more?"

"No, I..."

Without letting him finish, I slid over and hopped out of his truck.

I walked to the back of his truck, stewing over his words. Why was this so important to him? I didn't have to put up with this. Why couldn't he just be happy that I wanted to skip school to make out with him? Why would he care about anything else? What happened to the guy everyone said was just after one thing? Where was that guy? That's who I said yes to. Leaning against the tailgate, I wished I had just gone to school.

It only took a minute for him to get out of the truck, and walk towards me. Stepping to the side, I watched him drop the tailgate, and silently offer for me to sit. As I hesitantly accepted, he helped me onto the tailgate.

Standing in front of me, he questioned, "Why would you put up with someone doing that to you?"

"Why can't you just drop it?"

At first, Jackson appeared upset then his expression changed.

"Has anyone kissed it yet?"

I held my breath for a moment, shaking my head.

Hooking his finger into the front of my sweater, he asked, "Can I?"

"Why do you want to?" I questioned, not quite understanding why his question made me feel the way it did.

Stepping closer, he placed his hands on my sides. "'Cause when you're hurt, someone is supposed to kiss it and make it better."

I'd never heard of that before.

"Will you take your sweater off?"

Unsure of how to answer, I stared at him.

I really wanted to. I wanted him to kiss me, to make me feel better, and I knew it would. The problem was the dark bruise on my shoulder was only the beginning. If I took my sweater off, he would see all of the others sprinkled down my arms. What if he asked if there were more? What if he wanted to kiss them too? Or what if he looked at them in disgust, and thought I was weak?

Thinking of how it could go either way, and how neither would be good, I shook my head.

"Then can I take it off?" he asked as he slowly leaned in and kissed me.

He didn't wait for an answer this time. Continuing to kiss me, his hand from my side to the first button, and undid it. After making his way down to the last one, he stopped. He took a step back, and smiled before unzipping his hoodie. After taking it off, he tossed it into the truck bed, and stepped right between my legs.

My entire body tensed up as he placed one hand on my side, while the other held the top of my sweater on my shoulders.

"May I?"

I turned my head away from him, and closed my eyes. As I felt him pull my sweater down, I could feel his hand on my side stiffen. Imaging his expression, and what he must be thinking, provoked a sick feeling deep inside of me.

Ready to bail on him, I was surprised to feel a soft kiss on my shoulder. He removed his hand from my side, and carefully held my arm with both hands as he gently moved it around to kiss every bruise.

"I like your bracelet. Green is my favorite color," he whispered before taking my face in his hand and kissed my eye, again, before continuing to my other arm.

My chest felt warm as I opened my eyes, and watched his lips press against my bruised skin.

Jackson let go of my other arm, and ran both of his hands into the back of my hair, pulling it down. Wrapping my hair thing around his finger, he leaned in and softly kissed me. I felt close to him. The warmth in my chest invaded my heart before it spread down my arms, to my fingertips, giving me a chill. Smiling wide, Jackson reached over, grabbed his hoodie, and draped it over my shoulders.

"You should tell me who did that to you."

"Why do you need to know?"

"So I can stomp their ass into the ground, that's why," he replied, wrapping his arms around me.

"It's really not a big deal. I'm fine." I assured, sounding very much like one of those 'Social Awareness' videos they made us watch in middle school.

His gaze was pitiful, now. "This isn't the first time?"

"Are we gonna spend all day on this?"

"That's up to you."

Apparently, the fact that I wasn't confessing everything was irritating him.

"No it's not the first time, and I'm sure it's not the last time either. So, unless you want to take me back to school, drop it."

I could tell he was mulling over what I had just said.

Waiting to see what he was going to do, I seriously reflected on continuing to see him. I mean really, what was his deal? No one in my life had such a problem with this. Granted, he wasn't the first person to see a bruise, and ask a question, but his persistence was irritating. Why would he care that much? It wasn't like anyone was hitting him.

"It's not okay for someone to put their hands on you."

Giving up, I hopped down off the tailgate.

"It's not? Well, I sure wished I had met you sooner, because then I would have known."

"Wait," he blurted before I turned around, threw his hoodie at him.

"Who the hell do you think you are? I just met you, and already you think you have the right to tell me how things should be? You think I like having to wear long sleeves or missing school? Do you honestly think that I don't know how screwed up this is? Oh, but surely you bringing it up every five minutes, reminding me of what my life is really like, will make me feel better. I just wanted to hang out here with you, not feel bad about myself. Damn, why couldn't you just drop it?"

He stood there for a few minutes.

"I don't know why you would feel bad."

Teetering on the edge of assaulting him, I was ready to leave.

"That's right you don't. You don't know anything, and it's you that's making me feel bad and nothing else."

"You forgot your sweater." Jackson informed, still wearing his ridiculously expression of pity and confusion.

With a loud exhale, I stomped back over to the tailgate to grab it.

Quickly grabbing my sweater off the tailgate of his truck, it caught on the corner. Without thinking, I gave it a hard yank, tearing a big hole in it. Well, that's just great. I stood there staring at it. How was I supposed to go anywhere now? Glancing over, I saw Jackson hold his hoodie out to me. I stood there for a second before holding out my hand to take it. Pulling it back from my grasp, he shook his head, and held it open. Gritting my teeth, I stepped closer sliding my arm into the sleeve. Once I had it on, he reached down to zip it. Taking a step back, I grabbed the bottom, and zipped it up myself. At first he seemed disappointed. Then he smiled wide and held up his hand. My hair thing was still wrapped around his finger. Damn it, I needed that, too. I almost cracked a smile when Jackson held his middle finger up for me to take it back. I knew what he was doing, but I refused to endure anymore questions, or pitiful glances, concerning my situation.

Jackson stood there smiling and waiting. With a light sigh, I stepped in front of him. Taking his hand, I started to unwrap my hair thing from around his finger. Curling his fingers around mine, he tugged me a little closer. When I looked up at him, he leaned in, and kissed me. When he pulled back with a wide smile, I couldn't help smiling back.

"So are we good?"

"Yea, we're good."

"We still have a few hours before school's out."

"Okay, what did you have in mind?"

"We could get to know each other better."

His tone implied he was after more than conversation.

Raising an eyebrow, I informed, "I'm not sleeping with you."

"Good, 'cause I'm not tired."

Before I had a chance to say anything else, he lifted me up, and set me back onto the tailgate. Sliding his arms under mine, he pulled me against him as he kissed me.

The longer we kissed the lower is his hands moved, until they rested right around my hips. As his hands tugged me closer, the tension in my stomach grew. His polite persistence made me start to question how far I was willing to go. Then, as I felt his hand slide under the hoodie, I had to pull away. Smiling at him, I scooted back and crossed my legs in front of myself on the tailgate. Making his pouty face, he sighed.

He blew out a loud breath, while shaking his head, and set down on the tailgate next to me.

"Are you scared?" he questioned in a low tone.

"Of what?"

Rolling his eyes at me, he laughed, "Sex."

"No."

"Are you waiting?"

Trying to think of a good way to answer, I admitted, "Waiting implies that I'm waiting for something. I'm not waiting for anything. I'm just not going to."

"Not even when you're married?"

"I'm not going to do that either."

"Ever?"

"It just doesn't seem that great. I mean, why would you spend your whole time growing up waiting to be free, and do what you want, to get married and then always have to obey them?"

Jackson stared at me baffled for a moment.

"I don't think it's supposed to be like that."

"Oh, really? Then how come obey is in marriage vows?"

"Okay, I guess marriage isn't for everyone, but I still don't understand your aversion to sex."

This was not a hard concept to grasp, but I decided to explain myself anyway.

"My mother got pregnant with me so she and my father got married. For all I know, they were happy before that. They aren't happy now though. In fact, they're probably the most unhappy people ever, and if they hadn't had sex, she wouldn't have gotten pregnant, and they wouldn't be so miserable."

"What's your mom like?"

"She's not really like anything. She's just kinda there."

I could tell he was having a hard time understanding.

"And your dad?"

"My father," I corrected, "Is…unpleasant to be around."

There was a slight hesitation as Jackson imparted, "I see how you would feel the way you do, but I think you should reconsider the sex part."

I couldn't help laughing at him. "I bet you do."

"I'm being serious."

I laughed harder. "So am I."

"Well, what about everything else?"

Tilting my head to the side, I gave him a questioning look.

Leaning in, he kissed me before asking, "What about messin' around?"

"Nothing that leads to sex."

I started to get the feeling that sex was going to be an issue for us.

Staring back at him, I wondered how this was really going to work if we wanted different things. As much as I wanted for the issue of sex, not to be an issue, it was pretty clear that it was. It was unfair of him to try and change my mind on the matter, but in a way, I was doing the exact same thing to him.

"I like you," I assured. "But if this is going to be a problem, maybe it's better if we just…"

Jackson cut me off with a kiss before slightly fidgeting where he sat.

"Will you be my girlfriend?"

Caught off guard, that was the last thing I imagined him saying.

I nodded, leaning in to kiss him. "I really do like you."

"I really like you too." He assured before pressing his lips against mine.

I felt a little silly, but I couldn't stop thinking, I'm Jackson's girlfriend.

Later in the afternoon, it was time for school to get out. We headed to his parent's house. Quickly realizing he was serious when he said he didn't live far from the little wooded area, we were there in five minutes. I started to feel nervous, but when we walked in his mom was so welcoming I felt right at home. Her hair was strawberry blonde, and kept in a long ponytail. When Jackson introduced me, she seemed excited that my name was Ren, until I explained it wasn't like the bird, it was short for Rennillia. She then made my day by saying I must be special, because Jackson had never brought a girl home before. Not only did that make me feel good, but Jackson's face turned bright red, and he even started to twitch a little from the embarrassment.

Jackson's dad arrived when he got off of work. The four of us sat at the table for dinner. He was slightly taller than Jackson, and a little slimmer too. Aside from that, they looked very much alike, right down to their blond hair and smile. It was so nice having dinner with the Thomas'. The three of them kind of picked on each other, but in a very endearing way. It was especially cute, that they had nicknames for each other. Mr. Thomas was JP, short for Jackson Pierce, Mrs. Thomas was Suz, short for Susan, and Jackson was Jacks. Being around them was so different than anything I had ever experienced. I could tell, not only were they a loving family, they genuinely liked each other. When it was time for Jackson to take me home, both his parents hugged me, and said they hoped to see me again real soon. I wished I could have stayed longer. They were all smiles and laughs, and I knew that's where Jackson got his personality from.

Taking the opportunity to stop every chance he got, to kiss me, on the way to my house, Jackson caused a smile to be a permanent fixture on my face the whole way. When we pulled up in front of my house, Jackson offered to walk me in. When I declined, explaining it would be better not to, he seemed disappointed but understanding. After quickly kissing his cheek, I hopped out of his truck and strolled to my door. Looking back every few steps to see Jackson still there waiting to make sure I made it in safely.

To my absolute horror, my father was waiting for me. He opened the door before I had a chance to. My father glared at me first, then at Jackson's truck. I swallowed hard, mentally pleading just let me inside. I didn't care what happened after, as long as it wasn't out here in front of Jackson.

"Why are you wearing that again?"

A little relieved there was a reasonable explanation, I replied, "I accidentally tore my sweater today so I borrowed it."

"From him?" he growled pointing toward the truck.

When I nodded, he demanded, "Give it back, now."
Standing there wide eyed, I shook my head.

I heard Jackson's truck door slowly open. "I just have an undershirt on."

"Give it back or I will."

I breathed a weak, "Yes, sir," before turning, and walking back to Jackson's truck.
This couldn't be more humiliating.

I walked around to the driver's side, glancing at my father still in the doorway.

"I have to give your jacket back."

Stepping out of his truck, Jackson offered, "I'll go introduce myself, I'm sure…" before I stopped him. "Please, don't do that."

"Do you want your books?"

Shaking my head, I whispered, "I'm sorry," as I unzipped his hoodie.

I pulled it off and handed it to him.

Taking it from me, he held the side if my hand under his hoodie, whispering, "Get back in. We can go back to my house."

I shook my head and cringed, hearing my father shout, "Rennillia!"

I watched Jackson's eyes look me over as he pleaded, "I don't wanna leave you here."

With a slight shrug, I could feel tears welling up in my eyes as I turned and walked away.

Hearing Jackson's door close, I waited for the sound of him leaving as I walked back to my father. It wasn't until I was inside and the door was shut that I heard his truck drive away. I had only made it as far as the kitchen before my father grabbed my arm.

Pulling me around to face him, he growled, "Now he sees what you really are."

Without having a thing to say to my father, I gave him a dead stare. It appeared as though he was going to say something, then after looking me over, he let go of my arm, and walked away.

I heard his door slam shut, and my mother's open.

Walking up to me, she appeared distressed.

"Were you at the hospital?"

"No ma'am."

"When Scott got home from school he found Abigail…she took a bunch of pills…"

Standing there, I started to cry. I reached out to her, but she shrugged me away, and headed back to her room. No wonder my father was waiting at the door, he thought I was with Hert.

In my room, I quickly showered and put my pajamas on. Climbing into bed, I could only think of Hert. While I was laughing and having dinner with the Thomas', he was at the hospital with his mother waiting to see if she would make it or not. As I curled up in my comforter, I wished there was something I could do for him. Tossing and turning, I wanted to go see him. Finally, I decided if he was at the hospital with his mother, he would be okay until the morning.

Chapter 15

I couldn't wait to leave the house. Not as much to see Jackson today, but to find out how Hert was. My Father was awake and at the table. His expression was difficult to make out. When I walked past him, he turned his head in the opposite direction, refusing to look at me. I remembered hearing him yelling in the middle of the night, but instead of getting up, I pulled the covers over my head, and went back to sleep. Maybe my mother finally had enough of him, and told him off. My pleasant thought was quickly dispelled when he glared at me.

"I bet you think you're something, don't you?"

Confused, I shook my head. "Sir?"

"Go ahead, whore around with whoever you want. When you wake up on somebody's floor, it's your own fault."

I couldn't help making a face. "Sir?" I was completely baffled.

Jumping out of his chair, he reached to grab my face, then hesitated.

"You will still abide by my rules," He growled, pointing his finger in my face.

"Yes, sir," I replied, utterly confused.

Taking the opportunity to glare at me one more time, he sat back down when there was a knock at the door.

Turning towards the door, I rolled my eyes thinking my father may have finally lost it. It would be wonderful to think, after years of him trying to break me, I finally broke him instead. However, I already knew that wasn't the case, so I just went with my 'he's lost his mind' theory, and opened the door.

Emerson was standing there with a smile as he asked, "Ready?"

Nodding, I rushed out the door, closing it behind myself.

"Have you heard from Hert?"

"No, but I think he's alright. My father went to the hospital when he found out, to check on him. Hert spent the night at the hospital, and my father went back this morning. He said he would be at school today."

Em opened the door for me, and I slid in the passenger seat, breathing a sigh of relief.

I was happy that someone with the ability to help was looking out for Hert.

"That's really nice of your father to do that."

With a quick nod Emerson drove toward the school. "He likes Hert."

I couldn't help myself as I smirked, "Well, who doesn't."

"You mean outside of this car?"

Looking at each other, we both burst into laughter.

As our laughter subsided, he asked, "Speaking of people liking people, how are you and Jackson?"

I couldn't keep from smiling.

"He asked me to be his girlfriend, and I said yes."

"Awe you're in love."

"I wouldn't say that, but I do like him, a whole lot."

With an um-hum, Emerson pulled into the school parking lot.

Scanning the parking lot, I looked for Hert. With no sign of him, I smiled wide when I saw Jackson waiting for me. When Emerson parked, I hopped out of his car, and walked up to Jackson. The closer I got, the more I could tell he had an unsettled look on his face. Hoping that my father wasn't right about him seeing what I really was, I started to feel nervous.

I could feel myself frown as I stepped in front of him. "Hey."

Jackson's expression didn't change as he repeated, "Hey."

Trying to get him to smile, I asked, "Do you have class today? Or did you make a special trip, again?"

"I have class. Are you okay?"

Rolling my eyes, I insisted, "Yes. It was embarrassing but…"

"I wasn't trying to embarrass you or make you feel bad, I just didn't know what else to do."

Giving him a strange look, I assured, "You didn't."

"I was so worried leaving you there and…"

"Hold that thought, but I'm okay, really." I quickly replied when I saw Hert pull up.

The second Hert parked, I darted off to talk to him.

Making my way over, I thought about hugging him. Then as I got closer, I decided against it. Trying to get him to look me in the eye, I moved my head around until he stared at me.

"How are you?"

"I'm alright."

With a heavy sigh, I apologized, "I'm so sorry. I didn't find out 'til I made it home last night."

Hert's jaw flexed as he repeated, "I'm alright."

"Okay, I just wanted to make sure."

As I started to walk off, he asked, "I guess you're going to be okay, now?"

I quickly turned around.

"Uh, sure."

"I heard…" He started to say, then shook his head. "They're committing her."

My heart instantly sank. "Oh, no. Why?"

"She's sick."

"What are you going to do?"

"Mr. Roberts offered for me to stay with them, but my mother has some money in her account. I've been handling the bills since she went in the first time… I need to get a job, and then maybe just sell the house, and get an apartment."

"Why wouldn't you just stay with Emerson?"

"They were going to send my mother to a state institute, until Mr. Roberts stepped in. He made sure they didn't. That's already too much."

"Is there anything I can do?"

With a slight smile, Hert replied, "Yea, you can go back over there to your boyfriend before I have to kick his ass for glaring at me."

I smiled back at him, and nodded before walking back over to Jackson.

Emerson and Jackson were standing fairly close, and it was hard to tell if they were arguing or being secretive. When I made it right beside them, they were both quiet.

Emerson looked at Jackson and gave him a disappointed expression before turning to me and saying, "See you after school."

I nodded and tried to smile, but then I looked at Jackson. He must have decided to break up with me.

"Is there something you wanna say to me?"

"You're upset."

Rolling my eyes, I lied, "No. If you wanna breakup, you wanna break up."

"You wanna break up?" he questioned with a serious expression.

"Has everybody lost their mind today?"

Looking at me like I was the crazy one, he insisted, "I don't want to break up."

Before I could say anything else, he pulled me close, and kissed me.

His kiss was slow, deep, and incredibly inappropriate for the school parking lot.

"Okay," I breathed. "Why do you look like something's wrong?"

"Last night."

Tilting my head to the side, I consoled, "Nothing happened after you left. He just said now you could see what I was really like, but you already had seen, so...and then I went to bed."

Leaning against his truck, Jackson pulled me close to him. Hugging me tight, he quickly kissed my cheek. After that, his smile was back, and I was happy.

Unfortunately, the bell rang. Jackson and I had different lunches, which meant I wouldn't see him until the end of the day. Sliding into my desk, in first period, I noticed the two girls next to me were whispering. Normally, I wouldn't have cared.

Then, I heard one of them say, "Shhh, she's friends with him."

Listening intently now, I heard the other one whispering. "So. She's with Jackson, now. Anyway, my mom's cousin was in there, and she told my mom, Scott's mother flipped out and tried to stab the other nurse with the…"

I turned towards them, finding their conversation unbearable.

"You need to shut your mouth."

"Oh, I'm sorry. I didn't think you would care. After all, everyone saw you in the parking lot with Jackson this morning."

Giving her a dirty look, I snapped, "Excuse me?" as her friend turned, and faced the front of the class.

Then with a snotty little grin, she taunted, "But I suppose you do owe him. All that practice got you Jackson."

Smiling back, I assured, "Or maybe, not putting out on the first date, like some people…"

"Stand up!"

Facing forward, I realized, Mrs. Burnum was staring right at me. Thinking, 'damn it', I stood up.

Noticeably irritated, Mrs. Burnum stated, "By all means, share."

Smiling politely, I announced, "Yes, ma'am. I was just explaining to Lucy here, the benefits of abstinence while dating in high school."

With a heavy sigh, Mrs. Burnum fussed, "That's enough, Rennillia, and you know her name is Brendy."

Making a face, I questioned, "Really? Are you sure?" Then glancing at Brendy, I tilted my head and added, "Everyone I know calls her Lucy."

As Brendy started to cry, Mrs. Burnum snapped, "That's it! Out! Get your things and go outside the room until class is over!"

With a sigh, I slid my books off my desk, mumbling, "Yes ma'am."

I smiled to myself as I walked out of the classroom and into the hallway.

Standing outside of the classroom, I leaned my back against the wall, hugging my books to my chest. Wondering if what Brendy said was true, I thought, true or not she had no business talking about Mrs. Herterand like that. I had to mentally thank Hert for my little display in class. If there was anything I had learned from growing up with him, it was how to make someone feel bad.

Sighing with pride, over getting the best of that snotty girl, I saw Emerson walking down the hall.

"What are you doing out here."

Rolling my eyes, I replied, "I made Brendy Willers cry in class."

"You made her cry?"

Nodding, I stated, "She was talking mess about Hert's mother so I called her Lucy in front of the whole class."

Visibly trying not to laugh out loud, Em threw his hand in front of his mouth, making a little snorting sound.

Still quite proud of myself, I smirked as I questioned, "What are you doing out here?"

"My father called for me to come home."

"Is everything okay?"

"I think so, I'll be back to get you after school."

I nodded as he hugged me before leaving.

My next few classes seemed to drag on. I was happy when lunch rolled around, and I could see Hert. Standing beside him in the cafeteria line, I waited for him to get his tray. I looked up at him when he made an irritated noise.

"Come here often?"

Smiling, I felt Jackson's arms slide under mine, holding my back tight against him.

I tilted my head back to look at him. "Five days a week, from September to May."

"You're not eating? You want me to buy you lunch?"

"I haven't eaten lunch at school since the seventh grade," I shared with a laugh.

He let go, just enough to stand at my side with his arm around me.

Clearing his throat, Jackson looked over at Hert. "I'm sorry about your mom. I hope she gets better real soon."

At first, Hert narrowed his eyes then his expression relaxed. "Thanks."

Smiling to myself, I thought that was really nice, of both of them.

Jackson quickly kissed my cheek before he whispered, "I missed you."

Rolling my eyes and shaking my head at him, I smiled as I fussed, "Go to class before you get in trouble."

"Hands off the female students, Jackson," boomed from a voice behind us, causing the three of us turned around.
I wasn't as surprised by Coach Caffrey fussing at him as I was when Jackson grabbed me tighter.

"I just can't help myself."

Coach Caffrey laughed, "Boy get your butt to class."

"Yea, yea, do you still need me after school?"

"For about an hour."

Jackson nodded then kissed my cheek, again, before jogging off to class.

I stood there staring at Coach Caffrey not knowing what to say. Cleary, he knew Jackson, and was just messing with him. Now, I was left standing in front of him with my face turning red.

"You must be Ren."

Still at a loss for words, I blurted, "And you're Coach Caffrey."

Laughing at me, he shared, "I'm Carenza's cousin."
I shook my head, not knowing who that was.

"Susan…Mrs. Thomas…"

"Oh, it's nice to meet you."
As I looked at him, I noticed he looked an awful lot like Gus, minus the beard.

With another laugh, he assured, "It was nice to meet you too. You make Jacks behave himself."
Nodding, I smiled and watched him walk away.

Finally getting out of the lunch line, Hert and I found two seats in the corner. Watching him eat, I picked at the green beans he had at the edge of his tray.

"Why don't you get your own?"

Smiling wide, I confirmed, "Because I like stealing off your tray."
We both laughed a little, which was nice considering what he was going through.

Then, Mike Perdue walked up to our table. "Well aren't ya'll cozy."

Hert ignored him, continuing to eat as I stated, "We are, thank you."

"Jackson know about this?" he asked, trying to imply that I was doing something wrong.

"That I'm at lunch?"

Giving me a bad look, Mike snapped, "With him? I mean it's bad enough you're a…" stopping, as Hert stood up.

Hoping he would sit back down, I blurted, "Hert."
Mike turned to meet Hert as he made his way around the table.

Taking a breath, because I knew what was fixing to happen, I urged, "Hert, don't."

"Yeah Scotty don't," Mike teased in a made up voice.

Glaring at Mike, I assured, "I'm tryin' to help you out, stupid."

"Why? Is he crazy like his mother?"
At that point, all I could do was take a step back, and shake my head.

Walking up to Mike, Hert leaned in and whispered something to him. Mike's expression was instantly furious as he swung, and punched Hert in the face. Looking directly at Mike, as if his punch did nothing, Hert smirked, and raised his eyebrow at him. Mike started to swing again, but this time Hert caught the front of his shirt, and punched Mike four times in the face. With a heavy sigh, I walked around the table to Hert as he let go of Mike, dropping him on the floor. People were rushing over hollering, trying to help him up. Some were concerned, and some were shouting 'did you see that?' I have to admit, if you hadn't seen it before, watching Hert fight was pretty impressive.

We only made it a few steps when one of the teachers shouted, "You two! Principal's Office! Now!"
I glared at Hert, then followed him to the Principal's Office.

We sat there waiting to see the Principal for a hour and a half before Hert and I were called in together. Wondering why the two of us were being called in together, I hoped I was just there as a witness. The secretary led us in, then told us to sit, and wait again. Thirty minutes later, our Principal Mrs. Whimer walked in.

Wearing an irritated expression, she sat down behind her desk.

"You know, it's always the two of you. When one of you gets in trouble, the other's usually not far behind."
Adjusting myself in my seat, I sat up as tall as possible, and placed my hands in my lap.

"Both of you seem to be in the same trouble you're always in. Scott, you can't seem to stop fighting, and Rennillia, you can't keep your mouth shut. I'm guessing the fight was over Rennillia and your little display in class had something to do with Scott."
I couldn't believe Mrs. Burnum actually wrote me up.

Shuffling papers around, she continued, "Let's see, okay. Scott, you have got to stop letting people hit you in the face just so you can beat them up. However, since you didn't throw the first punch and in light of your current home situation, we're just going to let this go without punishment." Mrs. Whimer then looked at me, and shook her head. "I'm having a little trouble with yours. I understand that you made Brendy Willers cry."
I could feel Hert staring at me.

"It says here on your write-up, when asked what you were talking about, you stood in front of the class and said you were explaining the benefits of abstinence to Brendy, and then proceeded to disrespectfully announce to the class that everyone calls her Lucy."
All of the sudden I heard Hert start clearing his throat before coughing, then covering his face with his arms, and outright laughing.

Shocked, I fussed, "Hert, shut up."

Shaking her head at us, Mrs. Whimer questioned, "Why would you say that everyone calls her Lucy?"
Hert laughed even harder.

Finally, I watched her face turn bright red as she got it.

Pushing away from her desk, Mrs. Whimer stood up and fussed, "That's it, both of you out!" As Hert and I stared at her, she pointed to the door. "Out of my office now! If you two get in anymore trouble this year, I'll suspend you both!"
Quickly getting up, Hert and I hurried out.

Stepping out of the Main Office and into the hallway, I smacked Hert on the arm.

Still laughing and shaking his head at me, he gave me a little shove back. "I can't believe you said that."

"Well, she is. I can't believe you started laughing in Mrs. Whimer's office."

"I couldn't help it."

Mulling over our visit in the Principal's Office, I questioned, "I wonder if she kicked us out so she could laugh?"

"Probably,'cause that was funny."

"Hey, since we only have thirty minutes left, you wanna blow off last period?"

"Sure, I have to meet Mr. Roberts and his lawyer at the hospital to sign some papers anyway."

"You wanna wait with me outside until Emerson gets here?"

"He's not here?"

"No, he left earlier. He said he'd be back to get me."

"I'll wait until school lets out, then I have to meet Mr. Roberts."

Nodding, I followed him outside.

We stood outside by Hert's car until the bell rang. Watching students pour out of the school, Hert said he would see me at Emerson's later and left. I made my way over to Emerson's parking spot. It only took a minute before Jackson met up with me.

Jackson greeted me by pulling me into his arms and quickly kissing my cheek.

"You're not going to Roberts' house?"

"He had to leave earlier, but he's coming back to get me."

"Do you want me to wait with you?"

I wrapped my arms around him as I answered, "I want you to hurry up and get done at Coach Caffrey's so you can come see me at Emerson's."

"You do?"

"I missed you too."

Jackson's smile was incredibly wide as he pulled a black sharpie out of his back pocket.

"What are you doing?" I fussed, when he pulled the front left side of my sweater open.

Pulling the cap off with his teeth, he declared, "Claiming you."

"Claiming me?"

Jackson nodded, and wrote his name on the inside of my shoulder, right above my heart.

"As my own."

His words caused me to blush slightly. Whether it was things Jackson said or did he always seemed to get the best of me.

In an effort to have the same effect on him, I pulled the sharpie out of his hand, leaned forward, and wrote Ren&Jacks on the left inside shoulder of his hoodie.

"There. Now, I've claimed you."

I noticed him fidget, realizing after the fact, his was permanent and mine wasn't.

Jackson quickly kissed my cheek then wrapped his arms around my shoulders. "This was my favorite jacket."

I started to feel bad, but he didn't seem upset with me.

Then, I started to panic as he kissed me right under my ear, whispering, "But now, I think…I might love it."

I couldn't move or speak.

My mind raced and my heart was doing the same. Why did he say that? Was he putting it out there, hoping I would say it? Or maybe he was just reassuring me that he wasn't mad, I permanently marked his favorite jacket. I started to feel like I was going to hyperventilate. Thankfully, Emerson showed up.

I told Jackson I would see him later, without mentioning anything else. Hopping into Emerson's car, I couldn't help hoping the rest of my day would be a little less complicated. As we pulled out of the school parking lot and headed towards his house, I noticed Emerson looked not quite himself.

"Is everything okay?" I ask, already knowing it wasn't.

"My parents are moving to Spain."

"No." I blurted as my eyes welled up with tears.

"I really thought they were only looking."

"But I don't want you to go."

Emerson reached over and held my hand.

"I'm not."

Instantly relieved, I hugged his arm.

Then, the more I thought about it, I started to get angry.

"Wait, they're just going to leave you."

"Do you want me to go with them?"

"No, I just can't believe they're going to abandon you like that."

With a little smile he tightened his hand around mine, assuring, "My parents are not abandoning me. I'm almost eighteen, and Fidora is staying to look after the house."

Mentally disagreeing with him, I dropped it.

When we arrived at Emerson's, we waited outside the back door. I couldn't understand why he seemed so sad or why he didn't want to go inside. Sliding my arm around his waist, I leaned into him. Maybe, he wanted to go with them. I started to feel bad for needing him so much.

Looking up at him, I assured, "You won't be by yourself. I'll stay with you all the time. I'll even take turns with Helena."

His face fell and I knew what was wrong.

"We got into an argument, and she broke up with me. That's why I was late picking you up."

"What was the fight about?"

I never liked her in the first place.

"She said that I was wasting a great opportunity. That she had always dreamed of visiting Spain, and if I went she could talk her parents into letting her visit. I thought she would be happy I was staying."

Unable to help myself, I griped, "I knew it. I knew she was just using you. You know your mother didn't like her either and…"

Emerson stopped me, stating, "I know that no one liked her, alright."

Then it hit me, I was doing the exact same thing to Em that Hert did to me over Jackson.

"But you liked her. I'm sorry, Em."

"Yea."

"You'll find the right girl, and besides, you will always have me."

Looking down at me, he questioned, "Will I?"

I wrapped my arms around him. "I love you, Em, and I'm always going to be here, no matter what happens."

"I love you too, Ren," he replied, kissing the side of my head as he hugged me back.

Mrs. Roberts was seated in a chair in the living room. When we walked in, she politely smiled. Emerson and I sat down on the couch. Wondering why she was just sitting there, I noticed although there were no signs of crying on her face, there was a tissue in her hand.

"Rennillia, dear, we are having a dinner next Friday after Emerson's last game. Will you be able to join us?"

"Yes, ma'am."

"You are welcome to bring Jackson."

The three of us sat quietly in the living room until Mr. Roberts and Hert walked in the front door. Mrs. Roberts was instantly on her feet. I assumed she was going to greet Mr. Roberts then to my surprise, she stepped in front of Hert instead.

Placing her hand on his arm, she consoled, "Scott, I am terribly sorry for you," in a soft voice.

Hert's expression was reserved as he replied, "Yes, ma'am, thank you."
As she stepped away, his eyes revealed how stunned he was at her sympathy.

Mr. and Mrs. Roberts made their way upstairs, and Hert sat down next to me on the couch. I nudged him slightly hoping he would look at me. When all he did was scowl, I wondered if everything had finally hit him.

"Are you still alright?"

"Mr. Roberts offered me a job."

"A job doing what?"

"Stuff for the office, after school, and on the weekends."

"MR Industries?"

Hert started to nod before I heard Mr. Roberts say, "We best be on our way."
Hert stood up and walked toward Mr. Roberts. Without another word, the two of them walked out of the front door.

I looked at Emerson. "I don't understand."

With a slight smile, he nodded. "I never do."

Before I had a chance to ask him what his father actually did for a living, there was a knock at the back door.

Jackson strolled into the living room. Giving him the best smile I could as he smiled wide at me, I was happy to see him, but ready to have this day over with. Before he made it to the couch, Mrs. Roberts walked down the stairs.

"Jackson, will you be attending our dinner?"

Jackson gave her an uncertain expression, until I replied, "I haven't had a chance to ask him yet."

"We are having a dinner next Friday. Will you be attending it?"

After glancing at me, he replied, "Sure, okay. Yes, ma'am."

Mrs. Roberts gave a polite smile before informing, "Very well. I'll be back in a few hours, there is so much to do," and walked out of the front door.

I could feel Jackson staring at me as I looked at Emerson.

This was without a doubt one of the strangest days of my life.

"I'll be back down in a little while," Emerson shared before standing, and making his way up the stairs.

Glancing at Jackson, I mumbled, "I'm so ready to go to bed."

"I knew you would come around." Laughing as he sat down next to me.

Shaking my head at him with a smile, I assured, "Not what I meant."

Taking both my hands in his, he leaned in and kissed me before asking, "Did something happen?"

"A better question would be, what isn't happening. First, I got kicked out of first period. Hert got in a fight, and we both got called into the Principal's Office because Mrs. Burnum wrote me up. Then, Mrs. Whimer kicked us out of her office." I paused for a moment, purposely leaving out the part where Jackson himself freaked me out. "What's her face broke up with Em because his parents are moving to Spain, and he's not going. So he's all sad now. I get here, and Hert leaves with Mr. Roberts because he's going to work for MR Industries."

"I heard about what happened at school, but I didn't want to say anything in case you were embarrassed or somethin'."

"Why would I be embarrassed? People like Brendy and Mike need to learn to keep their mouths shut."

"It's good Hert was there to defend you."

Thinking he had the situation wrong, I snapped, "How was that good? I didn't need defending."

"Wasn't Perdue…"

"Giving me a hard time? All he was doing was talkin' a little mess, because I'm with you and I was sitting with Hert. I didn't need Hert to beat him up. For your information, I don't need to be saved, rescued or defended. I am perfectly capable of handling myself."

Jackson continued staring at me as if he wasn't quite sure what to say.

Holding his hand tight around mine, Jackson placed his other hand on the side of my face, and slowly kissed me.

Pulling away, he ran his hand gently down my arm. "Maybe you do and just don't realize it."

"No, I don't." I stated, on the off chance I had not been clear.

Swallowing hard and nodding, he kissed me. I felt bad for being that way with him. However, I did not want him to get the impression that I was weak just because he had seen a few bruises.

As usual, his kiss ended with wandering hands, and I was forced to blurt, "Jacks."

Making his pouty face before smiling wide, he swore, "I can't help it."

"We're on the Roberts' couch, and Em is right upstairs."

"Let's go for a ride then," he suggested, leaning in to kiss me again.

Shaking my head, I smiled. "I think we should stop for a minute."

"All I could think about at my cousin's house was kissing you."

"You're so silly."

"Hey, I have to go."

Instantly sad, I whined, "Uh, why?"

"Gus's wife had their baby today."

A bit more understanding now, I slowly nodded and forced a smile before he gave me a goodbye kiss that made me want to beg him to stay.

After Jackson left, Emerson brought me home. I wanted to be there for him, but I got the feeling he wanted to be alone.

Once I was home, I briefly thought of what Hert might do at MR Industries before coming to the realization that, in less than a year, we would all be eighteen, and things were already starting to change. Doing my best not to be severely depressed at the thought, I took a shower, and went to bed.

Chapter 16

Standing in my closet, I flipped through dresses. Trying to find one that covered my shoulder without having to wear a sweater was a bit difficult. The bruises that gave my arms a speckled appearance wear gone. However, the one on my shoulder was now an awful yellowish green. With a heavy sigh, I thought, 'why do we have to dress up for dinner anyway?' Mentally scolding myself for being that way, I decided I had no choice but to wear a little slate blue satin one with puckered short sleeves. It was slightly more fitted than I liked. It fell right above the knee, and from the waist up delicate ruffles hid tiny buttons. Hanging it on my doorknob, I set my strappy sandals on the floor under it. With another sigh, I sat down on my bed staring at it.

Over the last two weeks, I managed to convince Hert, Emerson, and Jackson that since I had never had a slumber party, we should have one when Em's parents left. Talking them into it was more difficult than I thought. After pouting when nothing else worked, the three of them gave in.

Hert was given the weekend Mr. and Mrs. Roberts were leaving off, so he could move also. His mother's house was up for sale, and Mr. Roberts signed for him to get his own apartment. Lucky for me, there was no way for Hert to back out of our sleep over because his apartment wasn't quite ready. He was staying the weekend anyway. Hert wasn't at all happy that I invited Jackson, but I figured he would get over it. So much was changing with Hert working, when he wasn't at school.

Most of my time was spent with Jackson, as he constantly tried to push the boundaries of our relationship. Happy to have dinner with Jackson's parents twice, the rest of our time was spent at Emerson's. Both Mr. and Mrs. Roberts were in and out of the house, and after much complaining on Jackson's part, over never getting to be alone, I worked out a solution. I picked a spot out on the roof that was easily accessible from Emerson's window, so Jackson and I could have a few moments alone. Sadly, my idea ended with Jacks tumbling off the side of the roof and into the bushes. I felt terrible, not because he fell, that was his own fault, because I couldn't stop laughing. Although he refused to set foot on the roof again, he was happy, I kissed his little scrapes and we were good.

Emerson seemed to be the most fond of my spend-the-night idea, and as it got closer he seemed happier.

I was going to Jackson and Emerson's last game of the season before dinner at the Roberts', so I went ahead and did my hair and makeup. I threw some clothes in my bag, and zipped my dress up in a garment bag. Carrying my stuff into the kitchen, I ran into my father. Disappointed he made it home before I left, I did my best to appear pleasant.

"Where is mom?"

"Not here."

"There's no school Monday, so I'll be home…"

"You will be home Monday night by ten and no later."

"Yes, sir," I agreed, already knowing that was what I had planned.

Then, as if he was angry at his own gesture, my father threw my car keys on the table. "There, now there's no excuse."

I started to say thank you, but I didn't get the chance. My father promptly gave me a dirty look, then stormed off to his room, and slammed the door.

Things with my father had been odd ever since he tried to shame me by giving Jackson his jacket back. Not that I was complaining, he hadn't laid a hand on me or even really spoken to me since then. All that transpired between us lately, were random gripes as he ordered me to do things. Which really made no sense whatsoever because every time, it was what I was already doing. In theory, my father could have seen what he had done to me that night and was sorry. In reality though, he had more important things to deal with other than me. His big investment that initially paid off was going under and that meant he was busy trying to make it work.

Either way made no difference to me, because I was going to spend three nights and days with Emerson and Hert. Jackson was getting to stay two of those nights with us. I was nervous about Jacks staying the night even though I had asked him to, and really wanted him too. Figuring with Em and Hert, there would be no alone time, I got over it, and was just happy we would all be together.

There was a knock on the door, and I rushed to open it, shouting, "I'm leaving!"

With no response from inside the house, I grabbed my stuff and headed out the door.

Emerson smiled, asking, "Are you ready?" as he took my duffle and garment bag from me.

Smiling back, I cheered, "Yes sir, I am. My father gave me my keys back so I'll follow you."

He seemed disappointed, but hid it well, because I was so happy. Placing my things in my car for me, Em gave me a hug and walked back to his.

When we arrived at the game, Jackson was already there, greeting us with his incredible smile. Emerson and I parked next to each other, getting out at the same time. He gave me a quick hug, and headed into the gym to dress out for the game.

Jackson made his way closer, asking, "Is that yours?"

"Yea, I got it awhile back, but then my father took it away."

"Not too bad, but I like it better when you ride with me."

"I do too." I agreed, thinking of being able to sit close to him with his arm around me.

"Wanna wear my jacket?"

Taking it from him, I slipped it on, saying, "It's my favorite too."

After giving me a quick kiss, Jackson offered, "We can share it then. It smells good after you wear it."

I had to look down at my feet to keep from blushing. The reason I liked it so much was because it smelled like him, and having him feel the same way, made my chest feel warm and my face turn red.

"I have to go in. Do you think we'll have a chance to talk to after the dinner?"

"Is something wrong?"

Shaking his head, he smiled. "It's more about things being right. But I really need to get in there."

Nodding, I kissed his cheek for good luck, and watched him jog to the gym doors. Turning before he walked in, he smiled wide at me as I gave him a little wave.

I stood in the parking lot for a few minutes, wondering what it was Jackson wanted to talk to me about. Until Mr. and Mrs. Thomas walked up. After hugs and greetings, they asked me if I would like to sit with them. As I happily accepted, we made our way inside. We found a spot for the three of us and as the game started.

Immediately, I started cheering for my two favorite players.

Looking around Mrs. Thomas, Mr. Thomas asked, "You like basketball?" with a wide smile.

Shaking my head, I replied, "Not really."

He made a strange expression before Mrs. Thomas nudged him, saying, "Honey, it's not the game she likes."

He gave her a blank stare at first then started laughing.

As the game continued, Jackson received a hard foul that sent him flying across the floor, and caused his mom and me to jump up and gasp. When it was clear he was alright, we sat back down, waiting for him to take his free throws. I watched him glance at us, and shake off a smile. It appeared as though he was trying to concentrate, but he couldn't keep from moving his shoulder up and down.

Leaning to Mrs. Thomas, I quietly asked, "Do you think he's hurt?"

Shaking her head, she whispered, "I think he's nervous."

Mr. Thomas broke in, disagreeing, "They're up by six and he can make these all day."

I couldn't see her expression, but I heard Mrs. Thomas softly comment, "You know he only does that when he's really nervous."

Not as quiet, Mr. Thomas questioned, "His twitchy thing…Why would he be?" then after a second, he blurted, "Oh…"

I was sure Mrs. Thomas had mouthed something to him.

Recalling the times I noticed him fidget, I asked, "He does that when he's nervous?"

"He used to do it a lot when he was little. We ended up sending him to a specialist. You know how mean kids can be. Now, he only does it when he's really nervous."

"Like, when you said I was special?"

Smiling, she replied, "Yes, but honey he's very self-conscious about it."

"Yes, ma'am, I won't say anything."

Mrs. Thomas was pleased at my comment, and I was more than pleased at his twitching. Whatever his reason for doing it now, was irrelevant. I made him nervous. When I claimed him by marking his jacket, and when he asked for me to be his girlfriend. I made him nervous.

When the game was over, I couldn't wait to see Jackson. Standing to the side, while Mr. Thomas recounted the highlights, and Mrs. Thomas looked him over, I waited for my turn with him. They told him that they loved him, to be careful, and not to stay out to late before hugging him goodbye.

The second his parents stepped away, I asked, "Are you okay?"

"You sound like my mom. Are you gonna wait for me?"

"I can't. I need to get to Emerson's so I can dress for dinner. I just wanted to make sure you were okay first."

Jackson kissed my cheek. "I better hurry then," he said with a wink as he headed to the locker room.

I stood there smiling for a moment until Emerson tapped me on the shoulder.

"Ready?"

He nodded, and we walked to the parking lot together.

The moment we arrived at Emerson's, we rushed into the house. Emerson handed me my garment bag, and carried my duffle upstairs with him.

The second Mrs. Roberts saw me she frowned. "You're not dressed."

I held my garment bag up, assuring, "I brought a dress."

With a sigh of relief, she asked, "I thought it would be nice to take pictures this evening, do you mind?"

"Oh, no, ma'am, I just need to change first."

"Of course, dear, you may change in the guestroom. It's next to Emerson's room."

I headed through the living room, wondering if she knew I stayed in Emerson's room with him. Otherwise, wouldn't I have known where the guest room was? Awful thoughts of what she must think of me formed, until I saw Hert.

Hert was sitting up straight with his hands in his lap, but his eyes were closed. Laying my garment bag across the back of a chair, I quietly walked up behind him. Finding it incredibly hard to resist, I threw my arms around his neck from behind.

"Wake up!"

He jerked before turning his face to mine, and smiling.

Out of nowhere, Mrs. Roberts snapped a picture. "This will be a good one."

Both Hert and I were startled. As I pulled back, I noticed, he was wearing a suit and tie. I waited for Mrs. Roberts to leave the room before walking around to face Hert.

"Well don't you look all spiffy."

Raising an eyebrow, Hert questioned, "Shouldn't you?"

I pretended to be offended with a slight huff. "I look good no matter what I wear."

Hert gave me a 'sure, you do' look before I stuck my tongue out at him, grabbed my garment bag, and darted up the stairs.

Standing in the guestroom, I glanced around thinking for such a big room it was awfully plain. I hung my garment bag on the closet door, and unzipped it, still wishing I had a different dress to wear. Once I put it on, I felt a little better. My dress was slightly shorter than I remembered, but the blue made my normally blah grey eyes really stand out. I looked around and remembered Emerson had my duffle with my makeup and shoes in it.

Outside Emerson's room, I knocked on his door.

"Come in."

Slowly opening his door, I walked in, asking, "Do you have my bag?"

Nodding, he complemented, "You look really pretty."

Smiling wide, I replied, "Thank you, you look very nice too."

After slipping his suit jacket on, Em left his room. I touched up my makeup, and added more hairspray to my up-do.

Sliding my sandals on, I glanced in the mirror one last time before heading to the top of the stairs. The living room was full this time. The Roberts', Hert, Emerson, and Jackson stood, visiting with each other as I made my way down.

In true Mrs. Roberts' fashion, Mrs. Roberts smiled, complimenting, "Rennillia dear, you are just lovely. Doesn't she look gorgeous?"

Feeling a bit put on the spot, I forced a polite smile.

Mr. Roberts was first to agree. "She always does."

His comment made me feel good about myself as I glanced over at Hert thinking 'see'.

Emerson was next, stating, "I told her she looked pretty."

Appearing put out, Hert quickly griped, "Yes," as if he felt he had no choice but to agree.

After, making a face at him, I looked at Jackson. There was no need for him to answer, I could tell how he thought I looked by the expression on his face. Slowly smiling, I made my way next to him.

Everyone, with the exception of Jackson and I, made their way into the kitchen. I stepped a little closer to Jackson's side.

Reaching down, I slid my hand into his, saying, "You look good."

With a serious expression, Jackson replied, "You...a... I'm kinda sore, and you like to hit."

Not being able to control my smile or the flush on my cheeks, I stepped in front of him. I slid my free arm into his suit jacket, and around his waist.

Leaning his head down, he whispered, "You wanna bail on dinner?"

At the moment I did, however, I forced myself to reply, "We can't."

"Let's go in with everybody else before I kidnap you then."

Smiling, I walked hand in hand with Jackson into the kitchen.

Dinner was pleasant. Mr. Roberts sat at one end while oddly enough, Hert sat at the other. Emerson sat at Mr. Roberts' right, next to his mother, and Jackson and I were on his left. Aside from Mr. Roberts sharing, he would be back down in a week for meetings, there was some small talk, but nothing important. Since they were leaving first thing in the morning, and it was already late when we started dinner, Mr. and Mrs. Roberts excused themselves as soon as Mrs. Roberts forced us to take pictures in various combinations. The rest of us stayed in the dining room. It felt grown up. While the four of us laughed a little talking about nothing, I wondered if it would be like this when we were all grown up too.

Glancing back and forth between the three of them, I couldn't imagine my life with one of them missing from it. A ping of reality struck me, and I started to feel sad. My countdown goal seemed to be working against me now. For the longest time, I couldn't wait to turn eighteen and graduate. Now, I wanted to hold on to what I had for as long as possible. I knew our time was limited.

Jackson nudged me, distracting me from my thoughts.

"Hey, I need to get going."

"Do you want me to walk you out?"

He nodded, and we stood up. Purposely avoiding eye contact as I passed Hert, I could feel his unhappy glare as Jackson walked behind me with his arms around my shoulders.

We only made it a few steps out of the back door before he pulled his jacket and tie off. Appearing happy to be rid of them, Jackson wrapped one arm around my shoulders as we walked to his truck. He opened the driver's side, and tossed the jacket and tie onto the seat. Turning to face me, he wrapped his arms around me, pulling me close.

"What time do you want me here tomorrow?"

"I think around noon would be good. What did you want to talk to me about?"

Taking a deep breath, he questioned, "Are we going to sleep together?"

Caught off guard, I started to pull away, fussing, "Seriously?"

Holding on to me, he clarified, "I mean in the same room, tomorrow night."

"I don't think that would be the best idea."

"Why not?"

He knew I slept in the same bed with Emerson before, but this was different.

"Because, you're my boyfriend."

As he nodded at me I could tell, although he was disappointed, he could see the difference.

Trying to make him feel better, I smiled before pushing up on my tippy toes, and kissing him. Jackson wrapped his arms tight around me as he purposefully kissed me back. Unsure if it was, knowing that I made him nervous, or the fact that he ask for us to sleep in the same bed with no reference to sex, his kiss felt different. It was making me lose focus. I didn't want him to stop. The longer he kissed me, the more it felt deep, meaningful and less like a means to an end. Before I realized it, my arms were just as tight around him, and I was pressing myself against him.

Keeping a firm hold on me, Jackson barely moved his lips from mine and breathed, "Let's go somewhere."

Whether it was his kiss, what he said, or the way he said it, my whole body warned me. It felt like I was being turned inside out.

Sliding my hands to his chest, I could feel how fast his heart was beating as I tilted my head away, urging, "I think we should call it a night."

"I a…I wanna say something to you."

Worried he was getting braver, since the whole jacket thing, I blurted, "Hey, I'll think about it, okay."

"Huh?"

Wondering myself, what I was thinking saying that, I replied, "Our sleeping arrangements for tomorrow, I'll think about it."

"Really?" he questioned with a huge grin.

Nodding, I gave a light smile. "Yes, but you need to go home, now."

Hugging me tight, he quickly kissed my cheek then my lips. As he let go, I stepped back allowing him to get in his truck, and close to door.

Standing there waving at him as he smiled wide, I thought what the hell am I doing? How could I even be considering this? Then, I reminded myself it was because he makes me happy, and I want to make him happy. Turning to walk inside, I thought, maybe this could work. My rule of no sex was not up for negotiation, but there were other things I might be willing to compromise on. After all, none of my flaws seemed to scare him in anyway. Satisfied with my decision, and still a bit tingly from his kiss, I pranced in the back door.

Giving me a dirty look when I walked in, Hert left the kitchen. Shrugging his shoulders, Emerson gave me a sympathetic smile as he and I made our way past Hert in the living room and up the stairs. In Emerson's room, I washed my face, and brushed my teeth. After thoroughly brushing out my hair, I grabbed my pillow, Jackson's hoodie, and a blanket. I hugged Em goodnight, and headed back downstairs. Not wanting the Roberts to get the wrong impression about me, I was sleeping downstairs on the couch.

I assumed Hert would take the guest room. Apparently not.

As soon as I saw Hert, I snapped, "I'm sleeping on the couch."

Without a word, he got up and moved to the chair.

Narrowing my eyes at him, I fussed, "There's no need for you to keep glaring at me."

"You need to stop and think about what you're doing."

"What am I doing?"

He looked at me as if he couldn't believe I was asking.

"With Jackson."

"What?"

"Look, Jackson's not a friend, but he's not a bad guy either, if he could keep his hands to himself, that is. I get that you're into him or whatever. Have you once stopped to think what being with you is going to do to him?"

I could feel myself frown. "What do you mean?"

"You know what I mean. He's not like us. He has a nice family, and whatever effect he has on you, you're going to have the opposite on him."

It was hard to argue with the sincerity in his logic, but I did anyway.

"You don't know that."

"Yes I do. Y'all have been together a few weeks, how many problems have y'all had so far? How many fights? And how many of those were from his side?"

I felt a little sick as the reality of his words invaded my self-esteem.

Lying down on the couch, I curled up in the blanket after zipping Jackson's hoodie around me. I wasn't sad because of what Hert said, I was sad because I knew what he said was true. Recalling the look on Jackson's face when he saw my bruises, how upset he was when my father made me give him his jacket back, each time he was unhappy. Aside from the misunderstanding on our first date, all he did was try to get closer to me. I didn't want to talk to Hert anymore about it, and even though I knew curling up with Emerson would make me feel better, I couldn't do that either. My relationship with Jackson was suddenly complicated, and I was no longer under the delusion that it would work out.

Chapter 17

At six thirty in the morning, Hert woke me from my not so restful sleep. I ran upstairs to brush my teeth, just in time to make it back downstairs before a caravan of people made their way into the house, and up the stairs to collect the Roberts' belongings. The caravan left, as quickly as they arrived, leaving Mr. and Mrs. Roberts standing in the living room to tell us goodbye. There were no hugs or I'll miss you's, only handshakes and polite nods. Then, they were gone.

I sat on the couch, looked at the clock, and noticed the whole process of the Roberts leaving only took an hour.
Glancing at Emerson, I asked, "Can I go lay down in your room?"
"Sure," he replied with a soft smile.
Slightly smiling back, I purposely ignored Hert as I made my way to Em's room. Curling up in his bed, I instantly fell back asleep.

Hours later, I woke fully rested just like every other time I slept in Emerson's room. I re-brushed my teeth, pulled up my hair, and changed my clothes. Carrying my shoes, and Jackson's hoodie downstairs, I looked around the living room. Finding it empty, I stepped into the kitchen and found Emerson and Hert sitting at the kitchen table.
Hert gave me a strange look as Emerson informed, "You missed breakfast."
"That's okay. Where's Jackson?"
"I'm going to pick him up in a few minutes."
"Why are you picking him up?"
"His truck broke down last night. He called this morning and said he tried to get it running, but the part he needs won't be in until Monday. I told him I would pick him up."
"Do you mind if I just go get him?"

Apparently my question made him laugh as he replied, "I didn't have my heart set on going."

"Can you move your car? You're behind me."

"You can take mine."

"Are you sure?"

Handing me the keys, Emerson laughed. "It's just a car, Ren."

I thought to myself, 'yea a really nice expensive car' as I took his keys, and ran upstairs to grab my bag.

Sitting down at the table, I slid my shoes on. Hopping back up, I thought picking Jackson up by myself might give me a chance to talk to him about our relationship. After what Hert said last night, I realized, I had way more to think about then our sleeping situation.

Before I made it out the door, Hert griped, "You're going like that?"

I glanced down at myself. "Am I naked and don't realize it?"

I could tell Em wanted to laugh as Hert fussed, "You might as well be."

Rolling my eyes at him, I knew my shorts were on the short side, but it was warm outside, and rare that I didn't have to cover up when going out in public.

"Did you give any thought to what I said?"

"Sure did," I spouted. "And the only one that has a problem is you."

I picked my bag up off of the chair, and walked out the back door.

I walked past the garage to the driveway and opened the driver's side of Emerson's car. As I slid in I admitted to myself, although I had thought about what Hert said, aside from feeling bad about myself, I hadn't put thought into it.

Taking the opportunity to think things over as I drove to Jackson's, I decided anything between me and Jackson should stay between the two of us. Hert may have been right, but it was none of his business. I strongly disagreed with his sort of relationship with Carmella, but aside from not wanting him to get himself in a bind with her, I didn't give him a hard time about it. Still, I couldn't get what Hert said out of my mind. Trying to shake off his assumption, that I was going to ruin Jackson's life, I hoped seeing him, happy, would make me feel more secure in our relationship.

Pulling into the Thomas' driveway, I was nervous. Remembering Mr. and Mrs. Thomas were leaving first thing this morning for an anniversary weekend, I hadn't thought about Jackson and I alone in his house. Taking a deep breath, I stepped out of the car, and walked to the door. Taking a moment to think, I decided the best way to keep things simple would be to catch him off guard for a change.

Ringing the doorbell five times in a row, I heard his muffled voice. "It's open!"

Smiling to myself, I continued to ring the doorbell as many times as possible, until the door flew open.

"Damn it Roberts, what the hell…"

Stopping the moment he saw me, I smiled wide at him. He must have been in the middle of getting ready. I couldn't help feeling a bit overcome. Jackson stood in front of me in a white wife-beater undershirt, basketball shorts, smiling wide with his toothbrush hanging out of his mouth. Why did he have to be so damn cute? I handed him his hoodie as he stepped to the side for me to walk in. He wrapped an arm around me and gave me a little squeeze. Shaking his head at me with a laugh, he walked back to the bathroom to finish brushing his teeth.

Sticking to my plan, I looked around and asked, "Oh, is that your room?" pointing to the little room next to the bathroom.

When he nodded, I chirped, "Okay, I'm going to go rummage through your belongings."

I didn't take the time to wait for his expression before I pranced into his room.

Giving his room a once over, I saw stacks of books in various places. There was a pile of dirty clothes in the corner next to an empty hamper, and his dresser was cluttered with papers and notebooks. He had a twin size bed that had a green and black plaid comforter bunched up on it. With no other place to sit, I decided if I made his bed, I would feel more comfortable being on it. After quickly tending to the chore he should have done when he woke up, I sat at the head of his bed. Glancing down at his nightstand that was also cluttered, I picked up a class ring brochure. At a different angle now, I saw a letterman jacket hanging on his wall by the door. One arm was covered with academic patches while the other basketball ones. It looked brand new, and I wondered if he had ever worn it.

Slipping off my shoes, I stretched my legs out in front of myself, I leaned against his headboard, and flipped through his class ring catalog.

"You weren't kidding," Jackson laughed as he walked in.

Glancing over at him, I noticed he had his hoodie on as I informed, "It looked like this when I came in. You're messy."

Flashing a smile as if he was proud of that, he blurted, "And you made my bed?"

I flashed a smile of my own, saying, "There is nowhere to sit in here. I figured it was better to be on your bed then in it."

Shaking off his smile, Jackson walked over, and stretched out on the bed next to me. Sliding his hand behind my back, he rested his head on my lap as he relaxed his other arm across my legs.

I had to hold my breath for a minute to keep from overreacting. It wasn't what he was doing that bothered me, it was the way it was making me feel. As I gathered my thoughts, I assured myself this was okay.

"Did you decide about tonight?"

Forcing myself to be honest with him, I replied, "I kinda got side tracked, but I'm thinking about it."

Nodding into my legs, I felt his fingers drag across my shin as he whispered, "Okay."

My stomach was knotting up, and I knew there was no way I could spend the night in the same bed with him and only sleep. I figured I could disappoint him later as I pretended to keep looking at the brochure.

"I've never had a girl in here before."

"Had or *had*?" I asked, trying to sound nonchalant.

Circling my knee with his finger, he whispered, "Neither."

Mentally pleading, don't do this to me I changed the subject asking,

"Why don't you wear your letterman?"

"'Cause I like my hoodie."

"Thought you loved it?"

I felt his smile on my legs, and decided to pretend I didn't just say that.

"So, you're getting a class ring?"

Jackson was back to brushing his fingers against my shin as he nodded.

"Which one are you getting?"

"On page four, ring 2a. Do you like it?"

"Aren't they all pretty much the same?" I asked, flipping to see the one he wanted.

"Yea, but you'll be the one wearing it."

"What?"

Sliding his hand up the side of my leg, he rested it on my stomach as he leaned his head back and looked at me.

Looking down at him, I couldn't make sound come out of my mouth. He was asking me to wear his ring months before he even got it. Why was he doing this? How long did he plan on us being together? How long did I plan on us being together? Not having thought of our future, at least not in terms of more than a week or two in advance, I knew we needed to talk.

Before I could discourage him from that kind of thing, Jackson offered, "Unless you wanted a promise ring or something like that."

I mentally shouted 'No! No! No!' as I whispered, "What would you be promising?"

Sliding up, so he was sitting next to me, he declared, "Everything."

My initial panic was instantly soothed as he softly kissed me.

Placing my hand on the side of his face as he pulled away, I breathed, "Jacks."

I meant to stop him, but when he pressed his lips back against mine, I didn't want to.

We sat there kissing each other for a while before Jackson started testing the waters. Starting at my side, he slid his hand under my shirt, resting it just below my ribs, without advancing further. For whatever reason, this made me want to mimic his action. I slid my hand into his jacket, and rested it on his side.

"It's okay." I whispered as he started to fidget.

That was all it took for Jackson to slide us both down, and pull me tight against him. Kissing me aggressively at first, it wasn't long before he slowed down. Softer now, he was barely kissing me.

His voice was low as he urged, "Please, I'll go slow."

I couldn't say no, and there was no way I could say yes. Then, out of the blue, Hert's suggestion popped into my mind. There was no way he would continue to tolerate this, and what if we ended up parting on bad terms because of it. If I did sleep with him and we broke up, it would be devastating. Desperate not to lose him, but unwilling to compromise or make him keep suffering though our relationship, I panicked.

Quickly thinking of things to say, I was confused and scared.

The only thing I could come up with to keep him was, "I think we should just be friends."

Keeping his arms around me, Jackson scooted back

"Are you breaking up with me?"

"Kinda."

"You either are or you're not. What's kinda?"

My eyes started to well up with tears. "It's just... I can't..."

"Don't cry. I'm sorry. We don't have to. I just got caught up, I guess."

Pulling away from him, I sat up.

"I can't be your girlfriend."

With a wounded expression Jackson argued, "You can't or you don't want to?"

"I like you, I really do but that is what you want and I don't."

"So."

Getting a better handle on myself, I imparted, "So, one of us is going to have to change to make this work, and I like us both the way we are."

Sitting up, he turned his back to me.

"You can go back to Roberts' now."

"You're not coming?"

Quickly on his feet, he questioned, "You still want me to go?"

"Yes, I really want us to be friends. I'll miss you if we're not, and besides this way we can hang out and have fun then you can go out on dates and do whatever."

Cringing a little at the thought, I wasn't ready for that, but if it meant we were still good, I could get over it.

Placing his hands on the sides of my face he asked, "Can I still kiss you?"

With a light smile, I nodded before turning my head and pointing to my cheek.

"Ah, I'm banished to the cheek."

"So are we good?"

"Yea, we're good."

Happy, I smiled wide.

On the way to Emerson's I thought about all the things I would miss about being his girlfriend. The more I thought about what all I would miss, the more I realized other than kissing him, it wouldn't be that different.

Breaking the silence of our car ride, I shared, "I'm glad you're good with being my friend."

"Can I kiss you?"

I thought he was joking at first.

"That would be inappropriate. We're friends now."

As I pulled up in front of Emerson's house, I realized he was serious.

"Just once, for old time sake?"

Looking at him, I hoped one day things might be different.

"Maybe later."

With a heavy sigh, he made a pouty face.

"Let's get drunk then."

I gave him a confused look. He pulled a bottle of liquor out of his bag, sharing that Gus had donated it to the cause as he slid it into the top of my bag.

Grabbing our own bags we got out of the car and headed to the doorway. As he reached out to place his arm around my shoulders, we both stopped and looked at each other. Both of us gave a slight laugh. Breaking our little habit of constantly touching each other would take some getting used to. I was going to miss that too.

The moment we walked in, Hert took one look at Jackson, and left the room. Rolling my eyes, and shaking my head, I watched Hert walk into the kitchen. Emerson took my bag, saw the liquor bottle sticking out, and gave me us questioning look.

"My cousin gave us a bottle so we could play up the river down the river."

"Up the what?"

Jackson laughed. "It's a drinkin' game…"

Then, we heard the back door slam shut.

Exhaling loudly, I glanced at the two of them and headed after Hert. Walking out the back door, I saw Hert sitting in the garage by the pool table.

"What is your problem?"

With a disgusted expression, he shouted, "You!"

"What did I do?"

"Just forget about it!" he snapped, getting up to leave.

Worried he was going to ruin my first real sleepover with friends, I shouted, "No! If you have a problem with me then I at least have the right to know why!"

"You know what, there's no problem. You can sleep with whoever you want."

I thought, 'thanks for your permission'.

"What are you talking about?"

I watched his expression carefully and realized how it must have looked.

"It's still none of your business, but I didn't bring Jackson so I could sleep with him. In fact, I broke up with him today."

"Then why is he here?"

"We're still friends Hert. Besides, I like him. He's not all cranky like some people. He's a lot of fun to be around."

He appeared offended. "Oh, so you like him better than me?"

Placing my arm around his, I assured, "I still like you the best. You're always going to be my favorite person."

"Really?" He looked down at me as if at this point he wasn't sure.

As I nodded at him, I heard Emerson call out, "Are ya'll playing or what?"

Letting go of his arm, I tilted my head towards the door, urging him to follow.

The four of us sat around the coffee table in the living room as Jackson passed out shot glasses, and pulled out a deck of cards, while explaining the rules of the game.

When Hert refused his, Jackson questioned, "You're not playin'?"

"Hert doesn't drink." I shared, giving Jacks a 'drop it' look.

Raising his eyebrows, Jackson shook his head and the three of us started to play.

I quickly realized, as with all card games, I was really bad at this one. I ended up taking shot, after shot, and even though I wasn't sure how long the game lasted, all three of us were tipsy towards the end. In my drunken state, I tried to stand up, and hit the floor.

As I laughed uncontrollably, Hert stood up and lifted me off the floor, fussing, "That's it. Time for bed."

Hanging onto his arm, I argued, "But I'm having fun."

"Falling on your ass is fun?"

"I guess not." I pouted before laughing again.

Hert started to walk me to the stairs, when Jackson blurted, "Aww, no goodnight kiss?"

Feeling myself smile wide, I let go of Hert.

"Maybe just one."

Stumbling toward Jackson, Hert grabbed me around the waist, stating, "Nope," as he lifted me off my feet.

"Sorry, maybe next time."

Jackson made his pouty face, and I started laughing.

"Look…isn't Jacks the cutest thing."

I patted Hert to get his attention. Grabbing me tighter out of frustration, Hert helped me up the stairs.

Almost at the top of the stairs, I glanced at Hert. He seemed so irritated and I couldn't understand why. Thoughts of how rare it was to see him smile provoked me to cheer him up.

Taking my free arm, I pulled myself in front of him. "Why are you always so grumpy?" I asked, and started to tickle him.

Caught off guard, Hert tripped and fell right on top of me.

With one swift movement, he jumped up, fussing, "Damn it, knock it off," and threw me over his shoulder.

Quickly taking me to guest room next to Emerson's, Hert dropped me on the bed.

"This isn't Em's room."

Trying to sit up, I could feel the room spinning.

I caught the side of Hert's shirt as he tried to walk away. "Stay with me."

Sitting on the bed next to me Hert shook his head as I pleaded, "I want you to stay with me, please."

I couldn't quite make out his expression as he griped, "Why did you have to drink so much?"

"You never stay, and I want you to."

Hert leaned a little closer. I heard him say something about wishing I wasn't drunk before I passed out.

Chapter 18

A few months after our sleepover, and many others, school was out, and it was summer time. Hert's job with the office kept him busy. He was barely around. I spent most of my time with Em and Jacks. Emerson was the same as always, a new girlfriend was in the picture, and of course he was in love with this one too. The only time I was unhappy was when Emerson and I went looking for Jackson, about a week after we broke up. We found his truck parked outside The Bar. I went in, and after his cousin Gus fussed at me, for coming in before I was eighteen, he informed me that Jackson was in the back and would prefer not to be disturbed. Sure he had a girl back there, I made Emerson take me straight home, and I cried all night.

Aside from that one time, Jackson and I's transition into friendship was effortless. There was constant flirting, on both our parts and we became good friends. No matter how much I enjoyed spending time with two of my friends, I still missed Hert. Emerson had a date with the new one, and Jackson I'm sure had a date with someone. With nothing else to do, I decided to visit Hert, and see his apartment. I asked several times, and always he said no, so I figured if I just showed up without asking, he had to say yes.

Hert didn't seem excited to see me, but at the same time, he wasn't mad either. He had no furniture. The only thing in his fridge was a loaf of bread, and a pack of bologna. It was clear, he needed help. There was no reason for him to be there all by himself.

Every day I came up with new things to borrow from Fidora to cook with. Until, I showed up, and she had a box of old pots, pans and dishes for me to take. We developed a routine of Hert leaving me money before going to work. I would hang out with Jacks and Emerson before stopping by the grocery store. Then, I would have dinner ready when

149

Hert got home. Although we slept on the floor in the living room every night, it was a lot of fun. I managed to stay there for almost two weeks.

I stood in the kitchen finishing up dinner, when he walked in.

"Smells good."

"It'll be ready in just a minute."

Hert stepped into the kitchen, assuring, "You're gonna make a good little wife one day."

"Do you want to get hit?"

"I think I could put up with some abuse if I got to eat this good every night."

"See, we should move in together after graduation."

Giving me a strange look, he asked, "You seriously want to?"

"Hell, yea. I mean you'd need a bigger apartment. I don't want to sleep on the floor for the rest of my life. We could have Emerson and Jackson over, and then nothing has to change."

With a serious expression, he asked, "What if it changed for the better?"

"How could anything be better than the four of us being friends?"

Before Hert had a chance to answer, his phone rang.

Hert had an odd expression on his face as he walked to the living room to pick up the phone.

"Scott Herterand."

He stared directly at me as he spoke.

"Yes sir... No sir... Yes sir."

Then, he held the phone out to me.

Confused, I walked over and took the phone. "Hello?"

Instant shouting caught me off guard as my father's voice questioned, "What the hell do you think you're doing?"

"Um..."

"You bring your ass home, now!"

Trying to resolve the situation, I assured, "I know I should have called, but..."

"Unless you want that boy to go to jail, you will leave now."

"Yes, sir."

I glanced at Hert.

"I have to go home."

"Are you in trouble?"

"He's probably gonna yell at me some more, but I'm not worried about it."

Hert stood in the kitchen, and watched me collect my things before I walked out of the door.

When I made it back to my house, my father was waiting in the kitchen for me. I set my bag on the chair before sitting down and waiting for him to let me have it for being at Hert's.

"What were you doing in that boy's apartment?"

"Cooking dinner."

Narrowing his eyes at me, he stated, "Don't be a smart ass."

Taking great effort not to roll my eyes, I assured, "I really was cooking dinner."

"What else were you doing?"

"I spent the day at Emerson's, and then went to the grocery store."

"What else are you doing for him?"

I couldn't help being offended. I knew what he was really asking.

"Not that."

Slamming his fist down on the table, he shouted, "Why else would he want you there?"

"I don't know."

After waiting a second for him to reply, I grabbed my bag off of the chair, and walked to my room.

I threw my bag into the corner of my room, and flopped down on my bed. Although I appreciated the fact that in the last few months my father managed to keep his hands to himself, I wished he could keep his mouth shut too. Kicking off my shoes, I curled up in my comforter. I was fixing to start my last year of high school and that meant I was almost eighteen. Hert would let me stay with him, if I wanted and after graduation, I never had to see my father again.

A knock on my bedroom door woke me up. Sitting up, I watched my mother walk into my room. She slowly made her way to my bed, and sat on the edge.

"Can I talk to you?"

I nodded, wondering what this was about.

"Your father means well."

Making a face at her, I shook my head. "No he doesn't."

"He's having a hard time. Nothing in his life has gone the way it was supposed to."

Lying back down, I stared at the ceiling.

"I know you don't want me to have sympathy for that man."

"I want you to think about what you would do, if you thought your life would turn out one way and…"

"I don't care."

My eyes started to water, and it made me even madder that she wouldn't look at me.

"You either make excuses for him or pretend like nothing's going on."

"I… I can't help it."

"Well, I can and I'm never gonna be like you," I swore before rolling on my side, and turning my back to her.

She sat on my bed for a few more minutes in silence.

When my mother finally left my room, I pulled my comforter over my head and started to cry. Upset with myself for expecting more from her than for her to be herself. I knew she didn't really care about me either. My father and mother were the way they were, and that was fine with me. They could do whatever they wanted with their lives, because I fully intended on doing what I wanted with mine.

Chapter 19

After spending the rest of my summer coming and going as I pleased, I planned to spend my last year of school exactly the same way. I walked off on my father while he was talking, left without permission, and stayed gone for days at a time without calling. Almost wishing my father would do something so I would have a reason to leave, I was now eighteen. The Roberts' would not be down until the week of graduation, and that meant no birthday dinner. Hert was of course working, and that meant no pond. Jackson took pity on me and planned a little party for me at The Bar.

This being the first birthday in the last three years that I did not have to dress up for, I threw on jeans and a t-shirt. With no hair appointment either, I pulled my hair up in a ponytail, and headed out of my room.

Skipping through the kitchen, I saw my father at the table and cheered, "See ya later."

"Where are you going?"

Shrugging slightly, I replied, "Out."

Giving me a resentful glare, he snapped, "You're going to wish you had minded me."

With a slight smirk, I sarcastically replied, "Thank you. I will have a good birthday."

My father sat there staring at me as I flashed a quick smile, and headed out the front door.

My first stop was Emerson's. When I arrived, he met me at the door with a soft smile.

"Happy birthday Ren," he greeted, and handed me three gold envelopes.

"What's this?" I questioned before stepping inside the house.

"It is a Society tradition. My mother suggested I do it."

Folding the envelopes in half, I stuck them in my back pocket before hugging him and saying, "Aww, thank you." Continuing through the living room, I walked into the kitchen.

Surprised to see Jackson there, he had taken an offer from Gus to help out at The Bar, on the weekends.

"Hey, I thought you would already be at The Bar."

"Nope, and I talked Gus into closing down early too."

"For me?"

"Turns out, Gus has a soft spot for the little dago girl after all."

Narrowing my eyes at him, I laughed. "Alright Paddy, don't start something you can't finish."

"Only 'cause you won't let me," he teased.

Instantly popping him on the arm, I blurted, "Jacks!"

"I have a present for you."

A bit surprised and excited, I smiled at Jackson as I watched him take his favorite hoodie off.

"Do I get to keep it?"

Giving me a strange look at first, he shook his head.

"You must be crazy if you think my jacket is your present."

Pouting a little, I urged, "You should give it to me. My name is on it and everything."

"So's mine. You're lucky we're friends, and I let you wear it."

"Yea, yea, so where's this present then?"

Smiling wide, he pulled a little box from the pocket of his hoodie.

Jackson handed me the little white box that was held together by a thin green ribbon. Raising an eyebrow at him when I shook it and there was no sound, I saw him smile wide. Pulling the little ribbon off, I set it to the side, and opened the box.

Inside was a green hair thing.

"Well, its practical," I laughed.

"I figured I would give you something you could use every day."

"I will think of you every time I pull my hair up."

Quickly kissing my cheek, he whispered, "I was thinking more, when you're pulling it down."

All the times Jackson kissed me, and slid his hands into my hair filled my mind. For a moment, I missed being his girlfriend.

Shaking off the thought, I gave him a little nudge, before walking to the downstairs bathroom. When I pulled my hair up with my new hair thing, I tilted my head around trying to see it in the mirror. Catching a glimpse of the green, I smiled wide before starting to feel sad.

There were only a few months left of the school year, and things were about to change. In my mind, they were not changing for the better. Jackson would stay through the summer, then he was off to college. Hert no doubt, would be working for the office full time. And Emerson, with no good reason not to, would probably be married in no time. With a heavy sigh, I stepped out of the bathroom trying not to dwell on the future.

Jackson and Emerson were waiting for me. Slowly smiling at them as Em informed us, for safety sake, a driver would take us to and from The Bar. We headed off to enjoy my eighteenth birthday.

We arrived at The Bar, and just as promised Gus had closed early. I felt a little uncomfortable at first. Gus was so different than the first time I met him. He seemed genuinely happy I was there.

After starting with several beers, it did not take long at all for us to progress on to shots. Laughing at Gus's stories of Jackson's family, and how Mr. and Mrs. Thomas met, I was having a great time. Gus made us all grilled cheese sandwiches just before his wife called for him to come home. Aside from Jackson and I throwing ice at Emerson, after he passed out, I drank enough not to remember anything else. Until, I woke up in the back room of The Bar with Hert sitting on the bed, appearing very angry.

My head was pounding, and I felt sick to my stomach. I started to sit up then changed my mind as a queasy feeling overwhelmed me.

"Are you about done?" Hert questioned as he glared at me.

"Done with what?"

"You are so irresponsible."

"Where are Em and Jacks?"

"I had the driver take them to Roberts' house."

"Guess the party's over."

"You need to grow up."

"What's your problem?"

Narrowing his eyes at me, he snapped, "I don't have time to baby sit your ass."

"Good, 'cause I don't need you to."

I forced myself to sit up.

"So this is what you want to do with your life?"

Almost tipping over as I stood, I steadied myself answering, "I'm not doing anything with my life, except maybe enjoying it."

"You were bad enough when you were getting your ass beat. Now, you're running around like you have no law."

"That's because I don't."

Shaking his head at me, Hert stood up.

"You need to listen to me."

He reached his hand out, and I quickly slapped it away.

"Why? So you can tell me how you think I should be? Why can't you just like who I am?"

"I never said I didn't like you."

"Could've fooled me."

Narrowing his eyes, he snapped, "You have no idea."

I threw myself back onto the bed, desperately needing to lie down.

"What are you still standing there for?"

Crossing his arms Hert made an angry noise before sitting down on the edge of the bed.

Still a little drunk, my head was swimming from arguing with Hert. I closed my eyes. So much for my birthday, eighteen was great for a few hours. Before falling asleep, I thought nothing was ever going to change for me, and the few things that would change, were things I wanted to stay the same.

Chapter 20

As graduation grew closer, the four of us spent less and less time together. Outside of school, I saw Hert about once a week. I still spent most of my weekends at Emerson's and had dinner at Jackson's twice a week, but it wasn't the same as those first few months after the Roberts' moved. Feeling our friendships slowly slipping away, I was more than happy when Emerson suggested we take a trip after graduation. It would be our last chance to be together before Hert went full time at MR Industries, and Jackson left for college. Because the reality of it was, the one thing I had waited my whole life for, was now something I dreaded.

Jackson and his parents were visiting the college he was going to attend for the weekend, and Emerson was locked into boyfriend/girlfriend activities, leaving me with nothing to do. I decided now was a good a time as any, to use my birthday present from Emerson, and his parents and get a new dress for graduation.

I flipped through dresses on the rack, not really concentrating on what I was doing. For a while now, some stranger had been showing up everywhere I went, with the exception of Emerson's and Jackson's. The first time he asked me out, I was at The Store with Emerson. After that, if I went to The Bar to hang out with Jacks, and help close it down for the night, he was waiting outside of it. If I stopped to get gas, he was there. I couldn't go eat, or even run to the corner store without hearing the same 'You should go out with me' from the persistent jerk.

Frequently glancing over my shoulder, I half expected to see my stalker. Then, a familiar voice came from behind that made me smile.

"That one's ugly," Hert shared.

Turning towards him, I laughed, "Well, at least I don't have to worry about us showing up to graduation wearing the same thing, then."

"Oh, ha-ha."

"What are you doing over here?"

"I'm off, and I needed to get a few things."

"In the girls department?" I teased.

"Shut up, I was over there, and saw you," he replied, pointing to the men's side of the store.

Laughing, I asked, "Did you find what you were looking for?"

"Not really."

"Me neither. You wanna go get something to eat? I've got three hundred dollars, burning a hole in my pocket."

"Sure, I'll drive."

As we turned to leave, I suggested, "Why don't we walk? There's a place to eat just down from here."
With a light smile he agreed.

While we ate, I tried asking questions about Hert's job. Other than him saying that he liked it, he really didn't say anything else. It was nice, just being the two of us. When we left, the restaurant we headed back towards The Store.

Then, while we were walking down the street, I saw the stranger heading our way.

"Uhhh," I groaned, turning to walk the other way.

"What are you doing?"

"That guy over there keeps asking me out. He shows up everywhere I go saying, 'you should go out with me'."
Scowling, he looked around.

"What guy?"

"Over there," I replied, motioning in my stalker's direction.
Hert appeared furious.

"You're not going out with him."
I was instantly offended that he was forbidding me to do something, and had to argue.

Before I spoke, I took a moment to stare at him as if he had lost his mind. "Did you just try and tell me what to do?"

"I wasn't trying, I'm telling you."

"Okay, let's just see how well that works out for ya."

"Damn it Renni." I heard him gripe as I walked away.

Hert had some nerve ordering me around.

I walked right up to him and smiled. He didn't smile back. Slightly confused at how someone as persistent as him could come off as uninterested in the midst of getting what they had spent so much time perusing, I decided to make the offer.

"Do you still wanna take me out?"

He narrowed his eyes, and looked directly at Hert.

"Yea."

"Then, let's go."

Before we walked away, I took the opportunity to glance back at Hert, give him a little wave, and a sarcastic smile.

Making our way past The Store, I realized, I had no idea where I was going or even the name of this guy. In an effort to make a point with Hert, I neglected to put much thought into what I was actually doing.

I looked him over as I shared, "I'm Ren."

"I know," he stated with a 'duh' expression.

I could already feel myself growing irritated.

"And you are?"

His tone softened as he replied, "Henley."

"Okay, Henley, where are we going?" I asked, trying to make light of how uncomfortable I was feeling.

Almost glaring at me, he questioned, "Ever been to The Diner?"

When I shook my head, he nodded. We continued to walk, and I assumed we were heading to The Diner.

Henley stepped into The Diner first, leaving me to open the door for myself then proceeded to sit down in a booth, and wait for me to join him. This was not going to end in anything other than aggravation. I could already tell as I stopped at the side of the booth.

Narrowing my eyes at him, I snapped, "Yea, I'm not staying."

For whatever reason, he appeared surprised I wasn't excited about this date.

"Why?"

Giving him a stupid look, I replied, "Um, because I don't even know you, and already, I don't like you."

He began to act put-out, like I was the rude one.

"Figures."

Now I was mad.

I took the seat across from him, in the booth, in an effort not to make a scene.

"What the hell is that supposed to mean?"

"Guess I'm not good enough for you."

"If this is how you're going to treat me, then you're right."

For a moment, he sat there just staring at me. Glaring back at him, I waited for the next idiotic thing to come out of his mouth.

Henley was rather plain looking. He had shaggy brown hair that almost covered his brown eyes, and rested right above his shoulders. He was average height, slim, but not unusually thin, just regular. It was possible I had seen him a thousand times, and never remembered him until he actually spoke to me because there was nothing outstanding about him.

I went against my better judgment, and decided to give him another chance. Maybe, he never expected me to say yes, let alone be the one to ask, and he was nervous. After all, my close friends could have been intimidating for him.

"I don't remember seeing you at school."

"How old are you?"

"Eighteen, I'm a senior. How old are you?"

With a relieved expression, he replied, "Twenty, I didn't go to school here."

"So… do you have a job?"

"I own a shop."

"What's it called?" I asked, thinking that was interesting.

Without expression, he answered, "Diavolo."

"What's your last name?"

"Medero. Why?"

"You know that means devil or hell depending on how you use it right?" I explained with a laugh.

Apparently, he didn't find it amusing.

Offended, he growled, "I know what it means and that's why I named it that."

Finding it hard to keep a straight face, I asked, "'Cause your shop is the devil?"

"No."

Unable to help myself, I questioned, "What sorta things do you sell in hell?"

Furious now, Henley insisted, "I get people what they need."

"So you're the devil?" I continued to tease before laughing so hard I couldn't catch my breath.

Henley promptly stood up, gave me a hateful glare then turned, and left me sitting in The Diner.

Ordinarily, I would have been upset that someone walked off on me like that, however, the whole diavolo/hell thing was so funny to me, it kind of cheered me up.

Two days later, I came home from school and found Henley sitting at the kitchen table with my father. Shocked beyond belief, I stood frozen as my father gave me a dead stare, while Henley wore a wicked grin on his face.

"You don't mind if I take Ren off your hands do you, Deangelo?" Henley asked my father, never breaking eye contact with me.

Stunned to hear the way he addressed my father, I actually gasped when my father replied, "If that's what you want."

I have to admit, I was in awe of him.

Henley stood up before giving me a slow blink. "How about it?"

I glanced toward my father as he got up, and walked to his room.

At a loss for words, I shook my head. "You know my father?"

Without answering, he bit the corner of his lip.

"I'll drive."

I nodded, thinking 'who is this guy?' before I followed him out of my house, and into his car.

As the shock of having Henley speak to my father as if he was the one in control started to wear off, I realized, I didn't know where we were going.

"Are we going to The Diner, again?"

"My house."

"For what?"

Giving me another suggestive smile, Henley replied, "I want to make up for last time."

I knew he was referring to what happened at The Diner, but I was unsure what his plans really were.

"What do you mean?"

"That's up to you. You're the one I'm making it up to."

"If you're trying to make something up to me then why don't I get to decide where we go?"

"Honestly, I know you're eighteen. I still don't want to take out a high schooler."

I saw his point, and at the same time, it occurred to me, he was a grown up. With a slight curiosity, and a hint of excitement, I quietly rode to his house with him.

We pulled up past a gate before he stopped the car. He didn't open my door for me, but he did wait on the driver side, until I made my way around the car and over to him. As we walked the path that led to his front door, I wondered what brought on his change in behavior.

Henley unlocked his front door, and opened it. I noticed right away, how clean the inside was. It looked like a brand new house. However, I knew by the way the outside looked, that wasn't the case.

"My your tidy," I commented.

With a serious expression, Henley stated, "I don't like mess."

I started to worry that between his mood swings, and obvious obsessive cleanliness, maybe he had some sort of disorder.

"So do you live here by yourself?" I asked, trying to get a handle on him.

"Yes. Sit."

I sat down on his couch, and watched him walk out of the room.

When he returned, he had a different shirt on. He sat down, uncomfortably close, turning his head to face me.

"These are your options. I can make you dinner, I can give you a present or…"

I couldn't stop myself from laughing. Was he serious?

"What?"

"My options? Really?"

Giving me a rather nasty look, he gritted his teeth.

Raising my eyebrows, I questioned, "Are you alright?"

Without answering me, Henley leaned so close I could feel his breath on my lips as he offered, "Or I can take you home."

I jumped up, unable to believe what an ass he was.

"What the hell did you ask me out for, if you obviously don't want to see me? Take me home then."

I walked outside without waiting for him to lead the way. I was furious. It felt like I was being played with.

The longer I waited outside on his porch for him to take me home, the angrier I became. It made no sense, I didn't even like him. Somehow, Henley managed to provoke an insecure feeling in me that only my father, and a few times Hert had. By the time he finally made it out of the door, I was wiping my eyes trying to keep tears from falling.

Henley stared at me with an indescribable expression on his face. He pulled my hands from my face, and pressed his lips against mine. Appearing as surprised as I was at the feeling, he grabbed hold of me, really kissing me this time. It was intense. I started to feel frantic. Far from gentle, he pulled me back into the house. Shoving me onto the couch, I should have cared, and it should have bothered me, instead, the way he handled me intensified the way his kiss felt. It almost felt like a fight. Every pull and tug was matched by a more forceful kiss, until my shirt was off, and I was pulling so hard against his, it started to tear.

"Is this what you want?" he questioned, pressing hard against me.

"No," I heaved out through heavy breath.

He didn't move.

"Are you with anyone?"

"No. But…I just met you."

The forcefulness from just seconds ago, still lingered on my lips as he slowly kissed me.

"You should be with me."

I tried to gather my senses.

"You might be the devil."

Sinister in expression, he suggested, "Don't put your shirt back on."

Stretching out on the couch, I watched him stand up, and walk to the back of his house.

He returned, carrying a shirt in his hand, and wearing yet another one. I couldn't quite put my finger on it, but there was something about him. He was rude, but at the same time he had these charming moments that made me want him. He handed me the extra shirt he was carrying before picking my shirt up off of the floor and folding it and setting it on the coffee table. Then leaning over me, he took my shoes off, placing them side by side next to his underneath the table. Moving my legs off of the couch, Henley sat down before pulling me onto his lap.

"Can I keep you?" he asked, brushing his lips against my neck.

Narrowing my eyes at him, I replied, "I'm not a stray dog."

He gave an irritated sigh, and glanced at the clock.

"Time to go home."

Taking a deep breath, I was confused. Didn't he just ask me to stay, and now he was shooing me off?

Slowly getting to my feet, I handed him back his shirt. He took it then leaned forward and kissed me from right above my belly button, all the way up to my chin as he slid his hands up my sides. Holding my arms up high as he stood, he looked down at me. Taking the shirt, he slipped my arms into the holes and then pulled it all the way onto me.

He leaned down, grabbed my shoes, and handed them to me. "Now you have to come back."

This man was so confusing. I wondered if maybe he just didn't know how to express himself.

A week went by, with no word from Henley. Preoccupied through dinner with the Thomas', even Jackson's smile couldn't fully cheer me up. I tried talking to Emerson, but all he said was that it was probably in my best interest not to see Henley again. Pulling up at my house, I saw a different car in my father's parking spot. Determined to ignore him, I crossed my arms and walked right past Henley as he stood in my driveway.

"Your father's not home," he informed as I reached the door.

Turning back, I took a few steps towards him.

"What are you doing here?"

"I came to pick you up."

"Oh, Really?"

With a slow nod, he stepped closer, and handed me a rose. "Yes."

Infuriated at his assumption, I fussed, "I haven't heard from you at all since I was at your house. You think you can just show up whenever you want?"

I could tell he was getting frustrated as he leaned closer.

"I was busy. You were with friends. Now we're both free. Let's go."

Holding my head high, I questioned, "Where?"

"My house."

In a huff, I shook my head and walked away.

"No thanks."

Quickly catching up, he cornered me by my front door.

"I've waited all week."

"For what?"

He didn't say anything at first then, as I started to open the door, Henley leaned closer. "You."

Having him stand close, not to mention how irritated I was with him, and feeling his breath on my face as he spoke, reminded me of the night at his house.

"I don't feel like going anywhere. But you can come in, if you want."

He didn't answer, he just stood there waiting until I opened the front door and followed me in.

Walking to my room, as Henley followed, I wondered what it would be like to have him in there with me. I was still mad at him, but I also wanted to feel the way I did at his house. It was better than drinking or even winning an argument. It was all action and no thought. I admit, it was

165

less about Henley, and more about the furious need he provoked.

When we reached my room, I opened the door. The two of us walked in before I locked the door behind us. I watched him glance around before glaring at Emerson's team shirt on my wall.

"Who does that belong to?"

With a slight smile, I informed, "Me."

"Who gave it to you?"

I set my bag on the little bench by my bed, and the rose he gave me on my nightstand.

"Emerson gave it to me to wear on game days."

"Where's mine?"

"Hanging in my closet."

In a rather demanding tone, he questioned, "How many boys have you been with?"

I didn't want to answer. For the first time in my life, my no sex rule made me feel less proud of myself, and more like a little kid.

"Does it really matter?"

His expression held a hint of disgust.

"You've screwed that many people?"

Well, that didn't come out the way I meant it to.

I stepped over to my closet. Yanking his shirt off of the hanger, I threw it at him before sitting down on the end of my bed.

"Time to go home," I spouted, giving him a 'yea you heard me' glare.

Without expression, Henley folded his shirt and set it on my dresser before slipping his shoes off, and setting them neatly in front of my dresser.

Biting the corner of his lip, he walked closer, leaning down, he assured, "Not yet."

It surprised me that he was refusing to leave.

"I said leave."

"Four." I shook my head not understanding, until he shared, "I've had four women."

"I don't wanna say," I admitted with a heavy sigh.

His smile was a bit disturbing.

"I don't mind if you're a little…"

I cut him off, because I had no idea what word was going to come out of his mouth.

"None. Alright."
I half expected him to make fun of me, but instead he shoved me back, and started kissing me.

This time hands wandered, however, nothing was removed. With a soft push, he adjusted me farther onto my bed. Pulling me against him as we faced each other, I noticed he looked like something was bothering him.

"Is something wrong?"

Shaking his head, he whispered, "I can fill in the gaps."

"What?" I asked, thinking that was a strange thing to say.

"When we have nothing else, we can have each other."
I felt the urge to let him have me. Staring at him, I nodded, thinking, there wasn't a more perfect thing to say to me. With my three friends preoccupied with their own lives, I would have my own life too. How could someone, I barely knew and hardly liked, know me so well.

I whispered, "Do you want me?"

"Right now?"

Stopping to think about it, I clarified, "Just in general."

"Do you want to check?"
My eyes grew wide. Before I could decline he laughed, and starting kissing me.

There were more whispers, and several kisses before I fell asleep. Unsure of what time it was I sat up realizing Henley had left. Glancing around my room, I noticed the shirt Em gave me was folded on my dresser, and Henley's shirt was pinned to my wall in its place. Shaking my head, I threw myself back, and gave a loud sigh before pulling my comforter over my head, and falling back asleep.

Chapter 21

The gaps, as Henley put it, seemed to widen as I spent more time with him, and less with my friends. It got to the point where everyone was miserable, including me. When I wasn't with Henley, all I could think about was seeing him. When I did see him, we argued about where I had been. Hert kept a constant anti-Henley position, while Em and Jacks complained about how I wasn't the same as I used to be. All I wanted was to be happy. None of them seemed to care. To make matters worse, I was seriously irritated that my father, of all people, was the only one not giving me a hard time. He didn't look at me or speak to me. It was like I wasn't even there.

On the way home from Emerson's, I stopped by The Bar to see Jackson, with the excuse of what time his parents wanted us at his house after graduation. It was going to be a full day. We had to get up, take pictures, practice walking, have lunch with the Roberts', graduate, go to the Thomas' for a party, then meet back over at Emerson's so we could leave first thing in the morning for our trip.

Truthfully, I just wanted to see Jackson.

The moment I walked in, I heard a Gus holler, "Hey girl, haven't seen you in a while."

"I know. Sorry." Instantly my mind drifted to shots, grill cheese sandwiches, and the night I spent an hour trying to say Augustus, but I was so drunk it kept coming out as Auggie-Gus.

Walking around the bar, Jacks smiled wide. "Hey, wanna give me a hand?"

"Sure," I agreed, following him to the back.

As we walked, I wondered what he wanted. When we reached The Dog House, he smiled and closed the door behind us.

"What?" I questioned, realizing he was up to something.

He flashed another wide smile at me.

"I was thinkin', since I'm leaving at the end of the summer, I thought maybe you could hang onto my hoodie for me while I'm gone."

Instantly my face fell.

"You can't have it. I want it when I come home to visit, but you know…"

Shaking my head, I could feel my eyes tearing up as I whispered, "I can't."

"You can't? Because of him?"

Shrugging, I couldn't answer.

"I thought it was your favorite, too," he griped before changing his tone. "It's all good, Ren, I'll just take it with me."

Thoughts of when I wrote our names on his hoodie, and why I liked wearing it, overwhelmed me. The difference between Jackson and I's relationship, and the one I now had with Henley hit me, and it hurt.

Unable to stand being in the spot where he took me on our first date, or see him smile at me, I turned and ran out. Using the back door, I didn't want to explain myself to Gus either. I made it half way to my car when Henley stopped me.

"I thought you were going home."

His questioning me immediately set me off.

"I can't stop and talk to my friend?"

"Were you talking?" he questioned, insinuating I was doing something else.

Insulted, I gave him a dirty look and turned to walk away.

He grabbed my arm, and growled, "Don't walk away from me."

Jerking my arm away, I snapped, "Let go of me."

Pulling me by my shoulders, this time, he ordered, "Don't."

I pushed him as hard as I could, shouting, "Get the hell off me!"

When I turned, to walk away, he reached out to grab my wrist, but caught my bracelet instead. Horrified, I watched it brake away and fall to the ground in pieces. Falling to my knees, I frantically picked up every bit I saw. Quickly getting to my feet, I shoved the remains of my bracelet in my pocket, said something very unbecoming to him, and drove straight to Hert's.

Furious the whole way, I couldn't wait to talk to Hert. Practically running to his apartment door, I knocked as hard as I could on it. After a minute, the door opened and Hert gave me curious look.

Marching straight inside, I asked, "What are you doing?"

"Wondering why you're here. What happened to your arm? And where's your bracelet?"

I pulled the pieces of my broken bracelet out of my pocket and set it on his bar. When I did, I noticed the bracelet must have cut me when Henley yanked it off.

Before I could tell Hert anything, he started yelling, "Damn it! See! I told you!"

"What did you tell me?"

"I told you not to go out with that bastard in the first place. You never listen to anything I say."

All of the sudden, I felt defensive.

"He didn't break it on purpose."

Narrowing his eyes at me, Hert questioned, "How did he break it then? Did he hit you?"

My whole thought process shifted as I fussed, "No, he didn't hit me. He's never hit me."

Hert let out a slight grunt in disbelief. "Yet."

Irritated by his assumption, I spouted, "Thanks for being a friend."

Walking back to my car, I thought Hert could be such a jerk.

On the way home, I started to feel guilty. I had told Henley I was going straight home from Emerson's, and I had in fact stopped to see an ex-boyfriend instead. Really, the moment I left The Bar and saw Henley, I was mad that he wasn't more like Jackson. I knew how insecure Henley was about all three of them. Remembering him telling me that he never knew his father, and he felt like his mother abandoned him when she died, I thought, he was just afraid of losing me. And, from what he described, the uncle that raised him didn't seem like a caring guardian at all. He did have some serious issues with possessiveness, excessive neatness, and the whole shirt changing thing still baffled me. I had my own things too, and we seemed to fill not only the gaps, but a void in each other.

By the time I made it home, Henley was there waiting for me. I sat in my car for a few minutes just staring at him, leaned up against his car, waiting for me to get out of mine. I didn't want to fight. Still upset over Jackson, mad at Hert, and absolutely devastated about my bracelet, I just wanted him to make it all go away.

The second I got out of my car, Henley was right in front of me, on his knees begging.
"Don't walk away from me."
He wrapped his arms around my waist.
"Stop, Henley, get up."
Holding me tighter, he shook his head.
"Will you leave me?"
"I won't. Please get up."
Finally, he got up. Leaning in, he kissed me.
When he pulled away, I asked, "Do you want to come inside?"
He shook his head.
"Do you want me to come to your house?"
He nodded, and I walked around to the passenger side of his car, and got in.

When we arrived, I got out as soon as the car stopped, without waiting for him to turn it off. After walking the path that led to his house alone, I leaned against his front door, watching him walk towards me. He unlocked the door before opening it. Inside, he stopped in the living room.
Turning towards me, he ordered, "Sit."
Shaking my head at him, I declined.
"No." I stated and, followed him into his room.
It was just as meticulous as the rest of the house. Reaching in his drawer, he pulled out a shirt.
I watched him pull the one he was wearing off before blurting, "Wait, what is that?"
Hesitant, Henley turned and raised his arm.

Starting at the top of his ribcage, there was a cross tattooed down his side, all the way to his hip.

Taking a step closer, I asked, "Is that for your mother?" Standing there, he quietly nodded. There was also a thick scar that ran from the top of the cross, through the center, and around to his back.

Reaching my fingers out, I brushed them against it. "What happened?"

Lowering his arm, he closed his eyes.

"I was sixteen. I didn't have permission."

I took a breath, and nodded.

"I have them too."

Shaking his head at me, he whispered, "You're perfect."

I wasn't, but at that moment I felt like I was.

Reaching my arms up, I wrapped them around his neck as he slowly lifted me up. Without kissing me he stared into my eyes as I wrapped my legs around his waist, and he carried me to the bed. Laying there with him didn't make me happy, in fact, the two of us were so sad it was almost depressing. Somewhere in my mind, I knew I would never forgive him for destroying my bracelet, but at the same time, forgiveness or even a genuine fondness for him seemed insignificant. He didn't ask to be forgiven. He simply asked for me not to walk away.

Chapter 22

Graduation day finally arrived. I found myself feeling better about it than I expected. Things were better since I spent the night with Henley. We came as close as possible to a real relationship with everything included as he circled the boundary of my no sex rule, without crossing it. He was more understanding about how limited my time was with my friends, and I was more considerate, making sure he knew exactly where I was at all times. I had one big blow up with Hert, Emerson, and Jackson. I explained that Hert had the office, Emerson had his girl, and Jackson had every other girl in town. Jacks came to my defense, saying I was right, and that as long as I was happy they should let me have something of my own apart from them. Finally able to create a balance in my life, all I had to do was finish out the day then, I would get to spend an entire week enjoying the friendships that were slowly slipping away.

Taking a deep breath, I stood in front of my mirror. My hair was straightened all the way down my back. Everything had been accomplished for the day, aside from, the party at the Thomas' house. I went between feeling like this was the end, and at the same time the beginning. I unzipped my gown and took off my cap, setting it on my bed. Laying my gown across my bed, I laughed a little, thinking of Jackson telling me it would be awesome if was naked under it. Shaking my head, I grabbed the bag I packed for our trip, and walked out of my room. I told Henley goodbye the night before, because he wasn't participating in any of the day's activities.

I stepped into the kitchen.
I shouted, "Bye," knowing there would be no response. Neither of my parents came to graduation. Why would they come out to wish me well on my trip? After waiting for a moment, just in case I was wrong, I continued outside, and

to my car. I placed my bag in the trunk before getting in and driving to The Thomas'.

Jackson's house was full of red hair, hugs, and giant smiles. Hert and Emerson stayed for about thirty minutes before heading to dinner with Mr. and Mrs. Roberts. It just so happened, it was Gus' birthday also, making the party even more eventful. After Gus hugged me, and thanked me for the wooden plaque that said 'The Dog House', he promised to hang it right above the door to the back room at The Bar. The more everyone congratulated Jackson, and talked about college, all I heard was 'he's leaving'. Not wanting to spoil anything for anyone, I smiled wide, and thanked everyone before heading to my car.

Almost at my car, the fresh air helped me get a handle on myself. When I started to get in, Jackson caught the door before I could close it.
    Standing back up, I smiled. "I figured since I'm gonna see you later, I didn't need to tell you bye." We both knew that wasn't why.
    "You okay? You haven't stopped shaking your hands or wiggling your fingers since you got here."
Looking at him, I felt the need to confess.
    "I miss you."
I wasn't sure if he understood what I really meant.
    "College doesn't last forever, Ren, I'm coming back."
    "What if you don't?"
    Stepping closer, he swore, "Why wouldn't I? Everything is here."
I had to look away so the tears in my eyes didn't fall.
    "Nothing's ever gonna be the same."
Jackson quickly kissed my cheek.
    "I have to get back in there…but…just don't do anything you can't undo. Okay?"
Nodding, I watched Jacks jog back to his door, before giving me a wink and a smile.

At Emerson's, Mr. and Mrs. Roberts congratulated me, again, before going to bed. I stood in Emerson's room, thinking he's gonna marry this one, and she's gonna take my side of the bed. I couldn't hold it in any longer. I started to cry. Actually, crying was an understatement. I wasn't ready. Not for our last week together, change, or anything that came after this day.

Hert asked Emerson to give us a minute. Em hugged me and stepped out of the room.

"Renni stop." Hert stated with an expression of genuine concern.

Shaking my head at him, I argued, "No, I can't. I can't do this, y'all are leaving me."

His tone grew soft. "No one's leaving."

"Jackson is."

With a heavy sigh, he agreed, "Okay."
He knew as well as I did, it was all falling apart.

Feeling the need to get everything off my chest, I cried, "And Em... He's gonna get married, I just know it. You're hardly ever around anymore. And you... Even you'll settle down, and get married one day. Then, you'll have your own family. I'm going to be left all alone with..."

Hert's voice was sober as he swore, "You're the only one I would ever marry. Renni, I..."
He stopped as Emerson stepped back into the room.

In the midst of my melt down, I heard the phone ring, but never expected it to be for me. Emerson held out the phone to me with a disappointed expression on his face.

Henley's voice was on the other end. "Hey."

"Hey," I breathed.

"Please come see me."
We agreed the night before not to see each other, until I got back, because I knew how hard it would be to leave him if I did.

"Okay."
I hung up the phone and quickly turned as Jackson walked in the room, smiling wide. His face fell as he glanced around and saw Emerson looking sad, Hert angry, and me, I'm sure regretful.

"I'll be back," I informed and started to walk out.

In an irritated voice, Hert announced, "She's not going."

Jackson's expression turned to worry as I shouted, "Yes I am!"

Scowling, Hert insisted, "No you won't."

Angry with Hert for calling me out, on what I already knew was true, I left the three of them standing in Emerson's room.

I already cried, and yelled, so by the time I walked down the path to Henley's door, there was nothing left but sadness.

He opened the door, took one look at me and said, "I got you a present."

Expressionless, I nodded. Carefully pulling up a chair, he walked me over, and sat me down in it.

"Eyes closed."

I couldn't get my friends faces out of my mind.

"Okay, open."

When I opened my eyes, I gave him a smile. In his hand was a gold bracelet with rubies, and diamonds alternating all the way around. I'm sure it was far more expensive, but it just wasn't the same. It wasn't once my grandmother's, or the only thing my mother did special for me, and it sure as hell wasn't the one Jacks commented on when he kissed my bruises.

Nodding at it, I pretended it was a worthy replacement. "Thank you."

Falling to his knees in front of me, Henley fastened it onto my wrist, saying, "Don't take it off."

"I won't."

He stood up, and pulled me to my feet.

"I have one more."

He reached into his pocket before pulling my hair into a ponytail with a red hair thing.

"Now you look like mine," he whispered into my cheek.

I had no idea he noticed that I always wore a green one.

"What did I look like before?"

"Someone else's with all that mick green."

Narrowing my eyes at him, I snapped, "Do you have a problem with Gus and his family?" Purposely not mentioning Jackson's name, I knew this was about him.

"No, it is fine for them. Not for you."

"Them?"

He looked at me like he couldn't understand what my problem was.

"Them. You know. Those..."

I stopped him, unable to think of one member of Jackson's family that didn't give me a warm and fuzzy feeling.

"Those what? You act like being Irish is a crime."

"Should be."

"Oh, I'm sorry. What do you do for a living again?" I questioned, suggesting he should rethink that comment.

Catching me by surprise, one of his hands was quickly knotted around the front of my shirt and the other was firmly holding my face.

"Don't ever compare me to a taig." Henley warned through gritted teeth.

Outraged, for so many reasons, I reached up slapping him several times, while shouting, "Don't you ever put your hands on me like that."

He let go, breathing heavily through his nose, he glared at me with his teeth clenched, watching me try to unclasp the bracelet.

I couldn't get the damn thing off.

"Don't take it off." He growled, provoking me to rip it off over my hand, and throw it across the room.

Instantly seeing stars, the back of his knuckles hit right under my nose as he back handed me. It took me a minute to steady myself. Shaking my head, I stared at him wide eyed as my nose started to bleed. It felt familiar, and I thought I was going to be sick. I pulled my hair down, flicked the red hair thing away, and turned to leave.

"You said you wouldn't leave."

He sounded wounded.

Furious, he was trying to make this my fault, I faced him, shouting, "I'm not leaving you 'cause I'm not with you! I don't even like your sorry ass!"

"I will come get you."

Done, I walked out then, ran to my car.

Wanting to get as far away from him as quick as possible, I sped all the way home. I couldn't calm down. When I made it inside, I grabbed a dishrag, and a hand full of ice before stomping to my room. I slammed my bedroom door. Instead of holding the rag on my nose as planned, I threw it against Henley's shirt that he hung on my wall, as hard as I could. I hated that shirt, and I hated him for trying to replace the people I cared about.

Yanking his shirt from my wall, I started to rip it apart when I saw 'don't leave me' written on my wall underneath. All of the sudden, I couldn't catch my breath. How did he know I would take it down? Holding his shirt tight in my fingers, I pressed it to my aching chest. Tears filled my eyes as I stood there shaking. I wanted him to come. Stumbling to my bed, I balled Henley's shirt up, and curled up in my comforter, holding it tight. I needed him. He could be rough or gentle, I didn't care. I just needed him to be here. I wanted to feel his breath on my face, to hear him whisper. The void he filled was consuming me, and I wanted him to be hurting too. He had to be. He said he would come.

Chapter 23

Whatever I felt the night before, instantly changed the moment I looked in the mirror the next morning. I had one dark bruise on each cheek that actually made me look like I had dimples, where Henley grabbed my face. My nose was swollen and under my eyes had a blue tint. It really hurt too. I couldn't do anything without my face throbbing. I spent the week in my room. I wasn't sad or depressed there just wasn't anything for me to do. Flowers arrived for me every day, and with every batch, I found new and interesting ways to dispose of them.

Henley and I were over and I was over it, but at the same time, I knew how my friends would react if they saw me. When Emerson called to tell me they were back, I was excited, but told him I would stop by in a few days, a few days and lots of makeup. When I finally did leave the house to go visit Emerson, Henley was waiting outside my house, when I left, and when I returned. Without looking at him or speaking to him, I just held my middle finger up to him each time.

I wasn't sure what Hert was doing, but he wasn't at Emerson's and I got the feeling he didn't want to see me. I couldn't really blame him. I knew he was mad and he had every right to be.

Jackson on the other hand was thrilled to see me. I think maybe he missed me, and it didn't hurt that Henley was no longer in the picture. I never said why we were no longer together, or why I never showed up for our trip, and Jackson didn't ask. There was lots of extra flirting and smiles from him.

Emerson was routinely disappointed over his latest break up, and the fact that I didn't want to stay the night. I missed him and visited every day, but my house was so peaceful, that's where I wanted to be.

My house was dead silent all the time. No one yelled or even spoke. I knew my parents were there, but I barely saw them. Each night before I fell asleep, I would smile at the spot on my wall where I wrote, 'Che Diavolo' over Henley's don't leave me. It seemed fitting that I used the name of his shop to tell him to 'go to hell' on my wall. Plus, I wasn't entirely sure, that if asked, my father would deny him access to my room. Most nights, I hoped he had seen it.

For several weeks, every time I saw Hert he refused to speak to me. I had dinner at The Thomas' a few times and even helped Jackson close down the bar on his last night working for Gus. Emerson practically begged me to stay the night. Finally, I agreed after he said Jackson wanted the three of us to spend the weekend together because he only had one week left before college.

When I arrived at Emerson's, Hert was sitting at the kitchen table.

"Hey." I greeted in a monotone voice.

Hert glanced at my little black duffle before asking, "Are you staying the night?"

When I nodded, he got up and left.

With a heavy sigh, I set my bag on the chair and sat down as Em walked in asking, "Where's Hert?"

"He left."

"What did he say?"

"He just asked if I was staying and then left."

With a soft smile, Em consoled, "Well, at least he spoke to you this time."

"I guess. When is Jackson gonna be here?"

"I thought he was coming tonight, but he has a date. He will be here tomorrow."

Disappointed, I stood up and walked to the living room.

I walked to the couch as Emerson followed. We both sat down.

"I still love you, Ren."

Leaning my head against the couch, I asked, "Why are you always so nice about everything?"

"I was upset, but I'm sure you were not purposely trying to hurt anyone."

"I didn't stay with him instead of going with y'all."

"You didn't?"

Shaking my head, I shared, "I guess, I was going to, but that's not why I didn't go."

For the first time since I met him, Emerson was blunt and straight to the point.

"You need to tell me what happened."

"Em... I..."

"Ren, it's important that you tell me."

Scowling at first, I took a breath and admitted, "If I had come back here when I left his house, the trip would have been ruined for everyone."

"Because you think we had a good time without you?"

Hesitantly, I explained, "Because...because I was hurt."

Emerson wrapped his arms around me.

At a whisper, he asked, "You're not going back are you?"

Shaking my head into his shoulder, I appreciated the protected feeling it invoked.

I have no idea how long I sat there with his arms around me. Feeling like I hadn't slept in months, I was so wrapped up in Henley, I forgot what this felt like. All kinds of things occurred to me and suddenly, I had a plan to make Jackson's last week before he left count, and find a way to get Hert to forgive me.

Pulling away, I hopped up.

"Let's go."

I headed out of the living room, through the kitchen and out the back door. Grabbing the basketball out of the garage, I skipped over to the court. Emerson's eyes lit up as I smiled, and tossed the ball to him. I spent so much time thinking about what I was losing, I forgot, Emerson was going to be all alone now.

After basketball, we played pool, then cards, watched a movie, laughed so hard I thought I would pass out, and finally went to bed. Curling up onto Em, I was glad to have my side of the bed back.

"Thank you," I whispered.

"For what?"

Giving him a squeeze, I replied, "For giving me a hug when I needed it."

"I love you."

"You're my best friend Em, and I love you too."

Closing my eyes, I recalled the first time I came to Emerson's house. I never would have guessed he would turn out to be my best friend. I smiled to myself thinking, and Jacks. No one thought we would go out on more than one date, let alone still be friends. And of course, Hert was mad at me, but then again, he always was. They were the most important people in my life. It was different now for all of us, but as long as I kept them my priority, change might not be so bad. My house and parents were different now, and it was a good different. Ready for the next stage of my life, I snuggled closer to Emerson, thinking we might be okay after all. Em tightened his grip on me, and I fell asleep happy.

Chapter 24

Fully rested when I woke up, I hopped into the shower. After drying off, and getting dressed, I wished I had packed something cuter for when Jackson came over. While I waited for my hair to dry, I sat on the edge of Emerson's bed, thinking of something to give Jackson before he left. There was only one thing he had ever asked me for, and I couldn't give him that, especially since he was leaving in a week. I decided to ask Emerson what he might like.

Emerson was standing in the doorway holding the phone out to me as I slowly walked towards him. I could tell something was wrong, but I couldn't figure out what it could be. When I put the phone to my ear there was a man on the other end of the line. He said there was a fire, and that he needed to speak with me in person about my parents.

Nodding into the phone, it wasn't until the man blurted, "Miss Cantinelli," that I realized I wasn't speaking.

"Yes sir, I'll be here," I replied before I hung up the phone.

I grabbed my bag off of the chair by his bed. Slowly making my way downstairs, I didn't understand what happened.

I sat on the couch in the living room waiting. When the Police Officer arrived, he had a Counselor and the Fire Marshal with him. The Fire Marshal explained what happened, using words like tragic and regrettable. The longer he spoke the less I heard, but when he used the word fortunate, I instantly hated him. The Counselor handed me a card and advised that I call her. The Police Officer asked Emerson if I had a place to stay. After Emerson assured, I could stay with him, they left.

Unable to believe what was happening, I just sat there. Feeling Emerson's hand on my shoulder, I turned and looked at him.

With more sympathy than I could have imagined, he whispered, "I am so sorry."

The moment I heard his sorry, I started shaking my head. I was sorry. Instantly, I wished I could take it all back. Every rule I broke, every sarcastic remark, every time I refused to submit to my fathers will, all of it. I wanted to take it back. I could have told my mother I understood, instead of wishing she was a different person. None of that was possible now, because they were gone.

Taking short breaths, I glared at Emerson.

"I should have been there. I didn't even want to stay here. I wanted to go home. I should have gone home. I should have been there."

Wrapping his arms around me tight, he soothed, "No, Ren, if you were, you would be gone too."

And then, I started to cry.

As my heaving sobs subsided, I couldn't look at Emerson. I wasn't mad at him. I just couldn't stand the pathetic way he looked at me.

Brushing my hair from my face, he whispered, "It is going to be okay. We will get through this."

Shaking my head, I pulled away and leaned the other direction.

"We will, Ren. I promise." I felt like I was going to throw up when he offered, "Do you want your pillow?"

"Yea, and the phone."

Em slowly stood up, and made his way up the stairs.

All I could think was, I have to get out of here, but I had no place to go. Not only were my parents gone, so was my house. Where would I go? Hert had already been through so much with his parents. How did he do this? He was strong and controlled through every moment of his father's death and his mother's breakdown. If I went to Hert, and he refused to speak to me or worse told me I needed to grow up, I couldn't handle it. Jackson was my only hope. He could take me somewhere, anywhere, so I didn't have to be here.

Emerson came back downstairs, handed me my pillow, and the phone before covering me with a blanket. Curling into my pillow, I dialed Jackson's phone number.

When Mrs. Thomas answered with a cheerful 'hello', I asked, "Is Jackson there?"

"No he's not. Ren, honey, are you alright?"

Trying not to fall apart on the phone with her, I replied, "I just really needed to talk to him."

I could hear the disbelief in her voice as she offered, "Okay, let me see if JP knows."
I held on the line while she asked Mr. Thomas if he knew where Jackson was.

"Sorry, did you try Gus?"

Disappointed, I answered, "No ma'am, I will."

"Okay honey, you sure you're alright?"

I lied, "Yes, ma'am."
After I called Gus' house, his wife suggested I call The Bar. Thinking, please be there, I dialed the number.

Gus quickly answered, saying, "Bar, what ya need."

With a controlled breath, I asked, "Hey Gus, its Ren, is Jacks there?"

"Was earlier, not sure where he ran off to."
I frowned at the phone.

"Okay."

"Ya want me to tell him you're lookin' for him if he turns up?"

About to cry again, I answered, "No, thanks."
Shaking my head into my pillow, I started crying as Emerson tried to comfort me.

Feeling as though I would die if I stayed at Emerson's any longer, I stared at my little black duffle bag sitting on the floor next to me. He wouldn't let me leave, I already knew it. I needed to be away from him, from this house. I didn't need comforting. I needed this to not be happening. I had to go.

Slowly sitting up, I placed my hand over Emerson's, asking, "Will you go get me my hair thing from your bathroom?"

"The green one?"

"I think, I left it on the edge of the bathtub this morning."

Giving me a sweet smile, he patted my shoulder, saying, "I will be right back."

Forcing a smile, I watched him get up and head upstairs.

The moment I couldn't see him anymore, I jumped up, grabbed my bag, and darted out of the back door. I had my keys out and in my hand before I even made it to my car. Quickly shoving them into the ignition, I left.

I must have circled the town twenty times before I finally pulled off to the side of the road. I felt lost. There was no place I could go. I understood there were actual places for me to go, however, there was no place I wanted to be. I didn't want to be told everything would be alright. Everything was not alright. It would never be alright, because my parents were gone. They were dead. The feeling of loss was overwhelming. I felt like I couldn't breathe. My chest was hurting, and I started to shake. There was no way to make this feeling go away. All I wanted was to stop feeling the way I was feeling. Then, I realized, there was a way.

Taking several deep breaths, I pulled back onto the road. Shaking my head at myself, I knew this was a bad idea. Suddenly goose bumps covered my arms in anticipation. Every reason not to go was quickly replaced with the way I knew I would feel once I got there. No thought just action. My sadness would be welcomed, and shared. Because when we had nothing else we could have each other, and I had nothing. There was never a gap like this in my life. He would fill the void that was slowly swallowing me whole.

Pulling up past the gate, I stopped my car. Slowly opening the door, it wasn't until I stepped out, I realized, I never put my shoes on. Carefully, I made my way down the path, mentally questioning myself with every step. By the time I reached my destination, I was severed into a million different emotions. The need for just one surpassed the rest. I closed my eyes, and made my decision. Slowly reaching up, I knocked on his door.

Life with HIM
A Companion Novelette
Rennillia Series
M. Sembera

Calmly opening the door, Henley looked me over. Before I could say anything, he shut the door in my face. I sat down in front of his door. Pulling my knees to my chest, I rested my head on them, letting tears roll down my cheeks.

When I heard the door open, I refused to look up.

"What do you want?"

Shaking my head, I wiped my eyes, saying, "They're gone. My parents are gone."

It was silent for a moment before Henley replied, "You left me."

"I don't have anyone, I'm an orphan. I don't have a family."

"What about your friends?"

Everything I was feeling reflected in his eyes when I looked up at him.

"I don't want to be with them."

"Get up."

Slowly, I stood.

Focusing on my bare feet, he snapped, "I can't let you walk in."

Frowning, I nodded.

Henley reached out, grabbed my arm, and jerked me towards the doorway. He leaned down, and lifted me up before carrying me into his house. Through the living room and into his bedroom, he stopped when we reached the bathroom. He set me down on the edge of the bathtub, pulled off his shirt, and folded it neatly before placing it on the counter.

"Don't leave me again. I need you," he swore as he knelt down in front of me.

"I won't," I breathed.

He nodded, appearing as sad and alone as I felt. I placed my hand in is hair, running my fingers through it. He reached his arms around my waist, and rested his head against my stomach.

"I miss the way I feel with you." I admitted, brushing my fingers against the side of his head.

"I miss feeling you," Henley shared, pulling me off of the edge of the bath tub and onto my feet.

Remaining on his knees, he stared up at me.

Henley's eyes never left mine as he unbuttoned my jeans, and slid them down my legs. My body hummed in anticipation as I stepped out of them. Every other thought was gone when he placed his hands on my hips, and sat me down on the edge of the bathtub. He reached under my legs, twisted me around, and flung my feet into the tub. I watched him carefully as he turned the faucet on, and gently washed my feet.

Starting with the top of my freshly washed foot, he followed my leg all the way to my hip with his lips. I closed my eyes as he continued up my back, taking my shirt with him.

"I need you."

My breath grew heavy as I turned to face him. When he pressed his lips to mine, I was lost in the feeling. All consuming, I willingly slid into the bathtub, pulling him with me. Heat and friction were all I felt, until I heard the crinkle of a wrapper, and then there was pain.

~L~w~H~

Alone in bed, I could hear Henley in the kitchen. He was cleaning. I assumed there are worse things to be obsessed with, even though, I still found it strange that someone needed anything to be that clean. Slowly, I slid out of bed. Not only was my body stiff and sore, but my heart felt that way also.

As I stood in front of the mirror in Henley's bathroom, I looked at myself. The hollow feeling inside showed in my reflection. I continued to gaze at myself, mortified by what I had done. It wasn't anything like when we messed around. It was invasive and I still felt violated, not to mention the pain that was involved.

I watched tears roll down my cheeks as I recalled Henley say, 'All mine,' when he stopped and looked between us, the moment the only promise I made to myself, ran down the drain. How could anyone want to do that? No matter how many times I had been hurt or injured, it was the single worst experience of my life.

Quickly wiping my eyes when I saw him step into the bathroom behind me, I wasn't sure what to say to him. I didn't know if he knew he was the reason I silently cried myself to sleep.

Turning me around to face him, Henley offered, "I can make you something to eat."
Shaking my head at him, I flinched when he pulled me to him by my hips.

"Are you sore?" he questioned with a suspicious expression.

"I need my bag."

"I put it in the closet. I'm going to the shop. I'll pick you up anything you need."

I started to say, "I'll just grab some clothes from…" with the intention of finishing with 'my house.' All of the sudden, I couldn't breathe. My house was gone, just like my parents were. Shaking and crying the pain in my chest was unbearable.

Henley slid his arms around me, holding me tight. I didn't want to be held. Squirming in his arms, I couldn't get away. The more I tried to break free the tighter he held me, until anger was the only emotion left.

"Let go!" I shouted, thrashing in his arms.
When he let go, I hit the bathroom door.

I yelled as loud as I could, "Get away from me!"
Henley raised his hands and I instinctively covered my face with my arms.

He wrapped his hands around my wrists, and pulled my arms away from my face. "I wasn't going to hurt you."

Shaking my head at him, I snapped, "I don't believe you."
Slowly letting go of my wrists, he walked out of the bathroom.

After standing there for a minute, I walked into his bedroom. He was sitting on his bed staring at the floor. Making my way right in front of him, I looked down at him.

"I didn't mean to hit you that hard," he said.

Confused, I questioned, "Why did you hit me at all?"

Keeping his eyes on the floor, Henley, replied, "I didn't want to hurt you. You were leaving. You wouldn't have come back."

"I wasn't gonna go. I mean, I was, but when you called, I wasn't."

Looking up at me, he shook his head, saying, "You didn't like the presents I gave you."

I fought back tears at the thought of my grandmother's bracelet.

"It wasn't what you gave me it's how you went about it."

"I had the night planned for us. I thought then even if you left, you would still be mine," he said before whispering, "You're my promised land."

Shaking my head, I stepped closer.

"Something that was saved just for me," he added.

Almost involuntarily, I slid onto his lap.

Henley wrapped his arms around my hips as I kissed him. I was wary of being so close to him after the horrific experience the night before. For some reason, my body seemed to welcome his touch, acting on its own accord. I closed my eyes and tried to relax, truly wanting it to be different this time.

~

Lying close to him, I kept my legs around his. It was more than just the high of coming undone, I actually felt like I belonged to him.

Recalling him say he needed to go to his shop, I asked, "You're not going to leave me now are you?"

Shaking his head with a serious expression, he replied, "Not ever."

"I meant to go to your shop," I said, smiling at his answer.

Biting the corner of his lip, he proposed, "I might close it down and spend all day every day in bed with you."

Tugging him closer, I kissed him.

~L~w~H~

We spent the next few days growing more familiar with each other. I discovered there wasn't much I didn't like when it came to the physical part. I also learned that his obsessive shirt changing was a result of the scar on his side. If he didn't constantly change his shirt while it was healing, it would stick to the wound. More or less a habit now, he grew uncomfortable if he wore the same shirt to long.

~

Standing in the bathroom brushing my teeth, I leaned my head to the side when Henley came up behind me. Sliding his hands under his t-shirt that I wore, I couldn't help pressing my back against him. After sharing good mornings, good afternoons, goodnights and 'it's been an hour let's do it again', my body practically bowed at the sight of him.

Disposing of the toothpaste in my mouth and my toothbrush, as quickly as possible, while still following his tidy guidelines, I turned and faced him.

Running my fingers into his hair, I pulled him to me and kissed him before saying, "Morning."

Pulling back, I noticed his unhappy expression as he informed, "Herterand needs to meet with you."

Instantly, my face fell as I shook my head and walked away from him.

Following behind me, he said, "I'll lay you out something to wear."

Quickly turning around, I fussed, "No you won't. I'm not going."

Shoving me back onto the bed, he hovered over me saying, "It's important."

I closed my eyes and whispered, "I can't."

Feeling his lips brush against mine, I pushed up towards him before he said, "You need to make arrangements for your parents."

My eyes filled with tears as I realized, it was my responsibility.

Nodding, I agreed asking, "Where?"

"Roberts'," he shared before pulling away and walking to the closet.

Scooting towards the end of the bed, I watched him lay the jeans and a bra he bought me on the foot of the bed before setting a pair of socks on top of them. I grabbed the bra and pulled my arms out of my shirt to put it on before quickly replacing the shirt. Lifting my feet one at a time, he slid my socks on for me. Appearing to take the matter seriously, Henley held my jeans to the floor allowing me to step into them. Once he slid them up and fastened them, he pulled me against him.

I nodded when he asked, "Are you wearing my shirt?"

"I still don't have shoes," I reminded.

Nodding at me, he replied, "I'll carry you to the car."
Turning away from him, I walked out of his room. Feeling as if I could start crying at any moment. I had trouble concentrating on what to do next. When I made it to the front door, I turned around and he was standing there with my keys.

Piggy backing me down the path to my car, I felt a little bad that he had to walk through muddy puddles from the rain. Henley opened my car door before turning his back to it allowing me to slide in without getting my socks dirty. I started to say something but decided against it when he continued to the house without looking back at me. Sitting in my car, I watched him all the way to his porch. After taking his shoes off, he stepped into the house, never looking back at me.

Driving as slow as possible to Emerson's house didn't achieve anything other than a few honks and dirty looks from other drivers. I still ended up in the last place I wanted to be.

Walking up to the back door, I knocked before the door swung open with Emerson on the other side, asking, "Why are you knocking?"
Shrugging at him, I saw my shoes sitting next to one of the kitchen chairs and my green hair thing sitting on the table. I gave Emerson a weak smile before sitting down and putting my shoes on. I was already feeling the need to run and I didn't want to forget them, again.

When I looked up from my shoes, Hert walked in. Just the sight of him made me cringe.

Serious and right to the point, he sat at the table and laid a packet down, stating, "We can start with your accounts then discuss..." before Emerson broke in, saying, "Give her a minute. She just got here."

"I can't stay," Hert stressed.

Glaring at Hert, I snapped, "You mean you don't wanna stay."

"I have to get back to The Office," he snapped back. Crossing my arms, I waited for him to say what he had to say then leave.

"This is the paperwork for your checking and savings. The insurance money is in your savings and interest dividends will be deposited into your checking once a month," he shared before saying, "Mr. Thomas is handling your account and Mr. Roberts has agreed to take care of the funeral expenses for you."

My head started to hurt as I narrowed my eyes and informed, "No funeral."

Confused, Hert questioned, "What?"

"No funeral," I repeated before sharing, "And if there is one, I'm not going."

I watched Hert's jaw flex as he stated, "Alright, then there is the issue of your residence."

My insides twisted as I yelled, "My house burned down, I have no residence!"

"You need a place to live," he shouted back at me.

"I am fine where I'm at, Hert," I spouted at him before he slammed his hands down at the table, fussing, "The hell you are."

All I could do was repeat, "I'm fine where I'm at."

Jumping up from the table, Hert yelled, "What the hell are you doing there with him!"

"You really want me to answer that," I spouted.

Visibly angry, Hert shouted, "What, now that your father's dead you wanna make sure he was right!"

Hert's comment cut me down to my soul as I stated, "I am fine where I am at."

After kicking the chair next to him, Hert stormed out of the kitchen and then the house.

I gave a heavy sigh and just sat there. Feeling Emerson's hand touch my shoulder, I hopped up from the table.

"I can't do this," I whispered, heading right for the back door.

Swinging the back door open, I started to rush out and ran right into Jackson. I glanced up at him before quickly making my way around him and heading to my car. I was almost in my car before Jackson grabbed the door and stopped me.

Finding it incredibly hard to look at him, I said, "I need to go."

"I am so sorry about your parents," Jackson consoled.

Nodding, I looked past him, saying, "Thanks, I really need to go."

Moving into my line of sight, he offered, "My parents said you can stay with them if you need a place."

Shaking my head, I stated for what felt like the millionth time, "I'm fine where I'm at."

"Ok, will I see you when I come home on break?" he asked.

Nodding as I looked away, I couldn't stand one more minute with him.

Quickly leaving after talking to Jackson, the sadness I felt turned to anger the closer I got to Henley's. By the time I pulled up past the gate, I was furious. Flying out of my car, I traipsed through puddles as it started to sprinkle again.

Flinging his front door open, I stomped in. The shock on his face from me getting his floor dirty with my muddy shoes caused me to lose it.

"Oh, am I getting your floor dirty?" I sarcastically questioned as I stomped up and down.

"Why are you doing that," he questioned, appearing hurt by my action.

Pulling my shoes and socks off, I threw them outside as hard as I could before running past him, shouting, "I told you I didn't wanna go!"

~L~w~H~

Only getting up to shower and eat a little, I stayed in bed crying and sleeping. I felt Henley come to bed each night but he didn't speak or touch me. I was so depressed I couldn't bare the thought of anything other than sadness.

~

After a few weeks, I was finally up and around. I slowly walked into the living room, seeing Henley sitting on his couch. Staring at him, he looked distressed.

"Hey," I said, meaning to sound more chipper than I did.

Scowling at me, he asked, "Do you need anything."

Nodding, I stepped closer before breathing, "You."
Yanking me onto his lap, he kissed me. Feeling something other than sorrow drew me closer. Wrapping my arms and legs around him, I laid my head against his chest.

"Sorry I stomped mud on your floor," I whispered.

Pulling my head back to look me in the eye, he said, "Anything for you."

The sad expression on his face caused me to say, "Do you need anything?"

"I get to keep you, that's all I need," he replied.
Recalling the first time he brought me to his house and asked me if he could keep me, I snapped at him that I wasn't a dog. This time, I was a stray dog. Without a home, I didn't even have shoes on when I wandered up to his door.

I didn't want to go back to bed but I wanted him. Wondering if he was opposed to venturing out of the bedroom, I pulled my shirt off.

Unable to decipher his expression, I assumed it was a no when he snapped, "Put your shirt back on."
Sliding off of his lap, I nodded before doing what I was told. I watched him standup and go to the other room. Thinking I had upset him, I sat there quietly waiting for him to return.

Henley walked back into the room. I noticed what was in his hand before smiling at him.

"Stand up," he stated.
I obeyed.

Biting the corner of his lip, he said, "Start over," sitting down on the couch.

Slowly complying, I anxiously awaited my reward.

~

Lying on a blanket, spread across the living room floor, I drew in a deep breath before propping myself up on my elbows.

"What if I went to the doctor and got on birth control?" I asked.

A look of disapproval spread across his face as he replied, "Why?"

Leaning my face closer to his, I whispered, "So we don't have to stop in the middle of what we're doing every time."

"Or so you can screw around and not get caught," he sneered back at me.

Shrinking back, I shook my head assuring, "I wouldn't do that."

"What would stop you," he questioned.

Pulling up, I swore, "I belong to you," before pressing my lips against his.

Rolling me over, he smiled reclaiming his territory.

~L~w~H~

Months went by. I had run into Hert while I was out a few times but the only real contact I had outside of Henley was Emerson. We had lunch in town. He was upset I didn't want to come to the house but Henley wasn't comfortable with my being there and honestly, neither was I. Missing Jackson's first visit home, I was guilted, by Emerson, into dinner at the Thomas' on his winter break.

~

Standing in the doorway of Henley's room, I stared at him sitting on the couch. It didn't matter that it was only for dinner, I knew he didn't want me to go. Walking over to him, I stood there, waiting for him to look up at me.

"You can say no," I offered.

Without looking at me, he said, "I shouldn't have to."

Sighing, I asked, "What do you want me to do? Emerson already told the Thomas' I would go."

Standing up in front of me, he griped, "Then go."

I started to say something then stopped as he turned and walked away from me.

~

When I pulled up at the Thomas' house, Jackson was standing outside waiting on me. It took me a minute of staring at his smile and willing myself to smile back before I got out of my car.

"Hey," he cheered.

Smiling back, I repeated, "Hey."

I started to step around him and go inside when he stopped me, asking, "So you're pretty serious with him?"

Finding it hard to answer, I replied, "I guess."

Jackson gave me a strange look before saying, "Ya'll are living together."

Nodding, I agreed, "I guess that is serious."

Laughing at me, he said, "You say it like you just figured that out."

Taking a moment to think, he wasn't wrong. I was so caught up in being with him, I didn't realize we were living together.

"I'm just staying there," I assured, feeling as if I had in some way betrayed myself.

A soft smile formed as he offered, "If you're just staying there, why don't you just come stay with me while I'm down."

Shaking my head, I thought 'Henley wouldn't like that' as I said, "Jacks."

Jackson took a step closer, saying, "I really miss you, Ren."

Before I could respond, Mrs. Thomas walked outside. Giving us a cheery smile, she walked over and hugged me.

I hugged her back before she pulled away, laughing, "I was wondering what was taking Jacks so long out here. Come on in, dinner's ready"

Happy for the interruption, I followed her inside.

Dinner was the same as always at the Thomas' table. Except now, I felt like I didn't belong. Smiling and laughing with them on the outside my heart was breaking on the inside. This was never my family and I would never belong here. I belonged with Henley.

After saying my goodbyes, Jackson walked me out to my car. I wanted our goodbye to be quick so I could leave.

"Let me know when you come down again," I said, opening my car door.

Holding onto the top of my car door, Jackson asked, "Do you wanna go somewhere?"

Caught off guard, I questioned, "Where?"

Smiling wide, he replied, "Anywhere."

Rolling my eyes, I genuinely smile at him saying, "Maybe later."

"I can wait," he assured, hanging onto my car door and smiling wide.

Laughing and shaking my head at him, I said, "I need to go."

Making a pouty face, he pressed, "Please."

"I can't," I said, unsure of how I was really feeling at the moment.

With a disappointed expression, Jackson said, "It is serious."

Shrugging, I replied, "We're still gonna be friends Jacks."

Nodding with a smile he agreed, "Always."

Suddenly my eyes felt watery and I needed to get away from him. Sliding into my car, I pulled the door away from his hands and closed it.

~

I sat in my car, staring at Henley's house, wondering why I came back. Conflicted and heartsick, I reminded myself Jackson was temporary. He was leaving again and Henley was always there. Henley was the only one there when I needed him. Everyone else had their own life and all he had was me.

Walking through the house, I was a little surprised that Henley was already in bed. Changing into one of his t-shirts, I made sure to put my clothes in the laundry basket before I slid into bed.

Reaching out to him, I whispered, "Are you awake?"

"Yes," he snapped.

Disliking his tone, I snapped back, "What the hell is your problem?" before practically flying off the bed and hitting the floor.

In the moment it took me to sit up and realize he shoved me off the bed, Henley was standing over me. Grabbing my arm, he drug me into the living room. Kicking my feet, the wood floor burned against my bare leg until I finally got my footing and stood. As soon as I did, he shoved me again. Holding my hands out to catch myself, I slid across the floor on my arm this time.

Listening to Henley's footsteps to his room before he slammed his door, I laid there. My father's voice echoed in my head, saying, 'When you wake up on somebody's floor it's your own fault.' Sitting up, I pulled one of my knees into my chest, wrapping my arm around it. Resting my head on my knee, I looked at my other arm and leg. Both with long red streaks and strawberry bruises forming, I wished I could go back and tell my father he was right.

Sitting in the middle of the living room floor, I started to cry. The pain from my arm and leg were nothing compared to the internal pain of regret.

I didn't notice Henley step back into the room until I heard him say, "Come to bed."

Shaking my head, I allowed my tears to continue falling. Feeling him carefully sit behind me, I tensed up. He slid his arms around my waist as his legs rested against the sides of mine. Flinching when he brushed against my hurt leg, I felt his breath at my ear.

"I was afraid you weren't coming back," he whispered.

Sniffling, I asked, "Then why weren't you happy when I got in bed?"

Dragging his lips down the side of my neck, he said, "You can't leave me."

"I'm not," I cried, still not sure what happened.

Pulling my head to the side, he assured, "I'll make it up to you."

Closing my eyes, I nodded, unable to control the feeling I had as he slid his hands from my waist to my thighs.

~L~w~H~

Henley did make it up to me and then some. There were flowers, new clothes, bubble baths and extra special attention every night.

~

Sitting on the couch, I waited for him to get home. I knew he would be late getting home from visiting his uncle but it was really late and I was starting to panic. When he finally arrived, I jumped up ready to fuss at him for having me so worried.

Taking one look at him, I frowned, asking, "Are you ok?"

Shaking his head, he walked past me and into his room.

Following close behind, I stopped him in the bathroom, saying, "Henley."

Looking at the floor, he shook his head.

Without thought, I knew exactly what he needed. He needed me.

Reaching up, I ran my fingers through his hair before sliding my hands down his shoulders.

"I'm a disappointment," he shared.

Gathering the bottom of his shirt in my fingers, I whispered, "Not to me," before pulling it off over his head. Folding it neatly, I set it on the bathroom counter. I ran my finger from his chest down to the middle of his stomach to the button on his jeans. Grabbing my wrist, he swung me around and pressed me against the door.

"Mine," he growled, letting go of my wrist and grabbing my hips so hard, I knew he would leave a mark.

~

I laid on top of him in the bathtub that was full of warm soapy water. Lifting strands of my hair before wrapping them around his finger, dropping them and repeating the action, he appeared content. The fury and aggression that he took out on me not even thirty minutes ago was gone. Even though it was rough, I knew he needed it to be that way. Knowing I was the only one that could make him feel better, made it more intense.

I knew I was going to be black and blue from the way he handled me, no amount of soaking in the tub would prevent that but I was hoping I wouldn't be sore in the morning.

Sliding me up to kiss me, he said, "I like knowing your mine."

"I am," I swore, pressing my lips against his.

Pushing me to a sitting position, he brushed his fingers against the marks he left on me, saying, "I like seeing where I've been."

Tilting my head to the side, I asked, "You like hurting me?"

"I like knowing you're mine," he repeated.

All I could say was, "I am."

And I was.

~L~w~H~

Time slipped by as everything but Henley slipped away. I still met Emerson for lunch once a month but most times we just ate in silence. Each time Jackson came home to visit, he joined Emerson and I for lunch because I couldn't deal with anything more. If I was away too long, Henley would get upset.

~

Surprised Hert was sitting at the table instead of Emerson, when I walked into the restaurant, I forced a smile and tried to make conversation.

"How's your job going?" I asked.

Keeping his jaw tight he nodded before asking, "Why are you still there with him?"

Finding it had been a long time since I asked myself that question, I shrugged.

"Take off your sweater its ninety five degrees outside," he snapped.

I could feel my hands starting to shake as I shook my head.

"This is what you chose?" Hert questioned, grabbing my arm and pushing up my sleeve.

Quickly pulling my sleeve back down, I took a step back, saying, "I'm fine."

"What the hell is the matter with you? Do you know what he says about you?" Hert griped before lowering his voice and informing, "The things he says you let him do to you?"

Crossing my arms in front of my chest, I suddenly felt exposed as I defended myself, saying, "That's private."

"You disgust me," he snapped.

Tears threatened my eyes as I said, "I thought we were friends."

"How could I be friends with someone like you? You're disgusting and I hate you," he declared.

Shaking my head as tears rolled down my cheeks, the only thing I could bring myself to say was, "Ok."

The anger and hatred in Hert eyes was too much for me to witness. Turning away from him I walked away, knowing I would never see or hear from him again.

~

Curled up in bed, crying, I felt betrayed. No matter what Henley tried, I refused to look at him.

"Tell me what I did to you," he begged.

Swinging my arms at him every time he tried to get close, I shouted, "How could you!"

"I don't know what I did," he stressed.

Without lifting my head off of my pillow, I said, "Because of you, he thinks I'm disgusting. You made him hate me."

Saying it out loud, brought me to terms with what happened and I let him slide against me.

"Who?" he asked.

Covering my face with my hands, I shared, "Hert said you told him everything we do."

I could hear the irritation in his voice as he questioned, "Are you ashamed of being with me?"

"No, I'm embarrassed. And he said he could never be friends with me now," I said, starting to cry again.

Pulling my hands from my face, he kissed my cheeks before questioning, "Herterand walks away from you that easy?"

"You shouldn't have told him," I snapped.

Sliding his hands under my shirt, he assured, "I won't do it again."

Henley kissed my neck down to my collar bone before making his way back up to my lips. Allowing the feeling to replace everything else, I slid my hands into his hair and kissed him back.

~L~w~H~

I was his and I did let him do whatever he wanted with me. It was just our way. Sometimes it got to be a little much for me but then sometimes it was better than anything else. I needed him just as much as he needed me. We needed each other and just like the times he understood, when I couldn't get out of bed, I understood when he got angry.

~

I shouldn't have said anything. I wasn't trying to upset him. Jackson had finally graduated and his parents were having a party for him at The Bar. It had been a long time since I saw anyone other than Jackson and Emerson and I really wanted to go. Holding the ice to my face, I was sorry I even mentioned it.

Sitting down next to me at the kitchen table, Henley took a piece of ice out of a bowl and rubbed it against my bottom lip.

"Is this better?" he asked, in a soft voice full of regret.
I nodded.

Glancing down at my bra, I saw a few spots of smeared blood on it before asking, "Am I still bleeding?"

Running his finger against my bottom lip, he answered, "No," before carefully kissing me.

Lowering the ice from my face, I asked him, "How do I look?"

"Sexy sitting at my table without a shirt on," he shared, placing the almost melted ice back into the bowl.

With a light smile I said, "Take me to bed."

Shaking his head with a sly smile, he stated, "Make me."

"Make you?" I asked, quickly realizing as bit the corner of his bottom lip, this was a game.
Slowly standing up, I slid onto his lap and kissed him.

Failing at making him take me to bed, I was more than pleased that he took me on top of his kitchen table.

Adjusting the blanket under us, I laughed, "You had me for dinner."

"You are dinner and desert all in one," he shared, hovering over me.

The table wobbled under us as I pulled him down to me, saying, "I want seconds."

"Careful, you might get fat," he laughed.

Sliding my arms around his back, I teased, "Only if you accidently knock me up."

Instantly his expression changed.

Climbing off of the table, he walked to his room. I gathered the blanket around myself before hopping down and heading to his room.

"I wasn't being serious," I assured, watching him get dressed.

Swiftly turning towards me, he grabbed the front of the blanket, twisting it tight around me, questioning, "You think that's funny?"

I frowned, shaking my head at him.

Grabbing my face with his hand, he growled, "I'm not enough for you?"

"I didn't mean anything by it," I swore.

Slowly releasing my face, he kissed me before informing, "I don't mind you staying here. Children are worse than pets."

Swallowing hard, I whispered, "I don't ever want kids either."

His expression softened as he shared, "You're mine. I won't share you."

Nodding, I tried to smile but tears rolled down my cheeks instead.

Lifting me up, Henley carried me to the bed. Carefully setting me down, he undressed before sliding into bed next to me. Closing my eyes, I felt him holding me close. I was serious about not wanting kids. I could barely take care of myself. Still, I couldn't help being sad. It had nothing to do with wanting more. After almost four years together, I was still just staying there. Not even a girlfriend or roommate, I was a possession.

~L~w~H~

Something changed in me that night. I willingly gave myself to him at a moments notice, I needed him but I no longer willingly gave up control. If he pushed, I pushed back. The fights were painful and the makeups were phenomenal.

~

I was shocked beyond belief when Jackson unexpectedly stopped by for a visit. As he knocked on the door, I silently debated if should answer it.

Shouting, "Just a minute," I ran to the bedroom and quickly got dressed before taking a minute to open the front door. Thoughts of 'should I', made me doubt how good of an idea this was. What if Henley came home and found him here? Deciding it was better to get rid of him before that could happen, I opened the door.

Slowly opening the door, I stepped out onto the porch.

"What are you doing here?" I snapped at him.

Looking me over, he replied, "I wanted to check and see if you were alright, Roberts said you were supposed to meet him for lunch and never showed up," before adding, "And you didn't come to my party."

"I just forgot about it?" I lied.

A familiar look from him caused my stomach to turn as he questioned, "Lunch or the party?"

Shrugging, I looked down and shook my head.

Taking a step closer to me, he shared, "You don't have to stay here. I can help you, just come with me."

"What makes you think I need help?" I snapped.

Narrowing his eyes in disbelief, he answered, "Look at yourself, why do you wanna live like this? I know it's always been like this for you but it doesn't have to be."

Jackson's reference to my father infuriated me and I shouted, "Just stay out of it! I'm fine here! I don't need you telling me what's best for me, just leave me alone," before slamming the door in his face.

Without watching for him to leave, I ran back to Henley's room and threw myself onto the bed. How could someone be that selfish? He didn't know what he was talking about. All Jackson ever cared about was what he wanted. He wasn't there when I needed him. When I needed someone, he was nowhere to be found.

~

Not quite over Jackson's visit when Henley made it home. I sat across the table, staring at him. Wishing I could scream and throw things. I wasn't willing to face the consequences if I did.

Henley placed his fork on the corner of his plate before looking over at me, asking, "Are you eating?"

Glaring at him, I stated, "No."

"Why not?" he snapped.

"I don't want to," I replied.

Narrowing his eyes at me, he asked, "Are you upset?" Without answering him, I got up from the table and walked into his bedroom.

~

Lying in the bathtub, I looked down at myself. I was still so angry with Jackson. How dare he come here and try to get me to leave. Who the hell did he think he was? He told me to look at myself. I was thinner than I can ever remember being and the fingerprint bruises down my arms, across my hips and thighs did make for a sickly appearance.

Looking up, as Henley stepped into the bathroom, I watched his eyes follow my body all the way from my toes before meeting mine. I didn't need anyone else.

~L~w~H~

When Henley said he wanted me in his shop, the thought of venturing outside the house with him was thrilling. On the way, he held my hand, leaning over and kissing me at every stop light. I was a little confused at first when we pulled up in front of a china shop but as it turned out, Diavolo was through a breezeway between stores, behind the storefront. Because of his dealings it was hidden so no one just ran across it.

Walking through the breezeway, Henley tightened his grip on my hand before pressing me against the wall whispering, "I don't know if I can wait."

Taking a deep breath, I smiled before saying, "So don't."

With a slight grunt, he kissed me before practically dragging me around the corner to the doors.

It was impossible to see into the shop through the mirrored glass doors. I caught a glimpse of myself as he unlocked the door and quickly looked away.

Pulling me into his shop, he locked the door before pressing me against it, stating, "I need you."

Gathering his shirt in my fingers, I panted, "Now," unable to control myself.

I didn't even get his shirt all the way off before there was a tap on the glass behind us.

Banished to the back room, every time I thought we would have a minute, the phone rang or there was another knock at the door. Sitting on a table in the back room, I rolled my eyes and gave a heavy sigh each time he stepped in and then right back out. Frustrated and bored out of my mind, I spent the entire day in hell.

~

Henley stepped into the room. The look in his eyes was all the confirmation I needed that his shop was finally closed.

Leaning over to kiss me, I pulled away, griping, "I'm so glad I came. This was so much better than spending the day by myself."

"I was busy," he defended.

Rolling my eyes, I hopped off the table.

Pushing me into the table, he whispered, "Shop's closed now."

Flicking the buttons open on my shirt, he kissed all the way to my belly button.

Watching him make his way back up my stomach to my lips, I pouted, "You left me back here all by myself."

"I neglected you," he admitted.

As I nodded at him, he seemed genuinely upset by what I said.

Falling to his knees, Henley stared at the floor. Slowly pulling me down with him, his every movement was completely devoted to my fulfillment.

~L~w~H~

Shivering on the edge of the bathtub, I watched him turn the faucet on. The same morose expression on his face as always, he wouldn't look at me. It even hurt to breath. I didn't want to take a bath. I wanted to go to sleep. At the moment, I couldn't even remember what started the fight in the first place. All I knew was this was the worst fight we ever had.

I slid into the warm water and it burned. Tears, that refused to subside, poured down my cheeks. Looking at

Henley sitting on the bathroom floor staring at the wall instead of me, I knew it was bad.

Taking slow shallow breaths, I asked, "Are you ok?"

"I didn't mean to hurt you that bad," he mumbled.

Nodding, I consoled, "I know," before saying, "Look at me."

His breath grew heavy as he narrowed his eyes at me, swearing, "I will take care of you until you get better."

"I wanna get out," I said before noticing his expression and clarifying, "Out of the tub."

Slowly standing up, he grabbed a towel and lifted me out of the bathtub.

Finding it hard to stand on my own, I held onto his arm as he carefully dried me off. Every time I tried to glance at myself in the mirror, he moved blocking my view.

Helping me to the bed, he questioned, "Why did you make me do this to you?"

"I'm sorry," I whispered, wondering why myself.

My father always said I didn't know my place. What was wrong with me?

As he slowly pulled the covers over me, I assured, "I need you."

Sliding into bed next to me, he pulled my back against him, saying, "I'll be gentle."

~

Henley fell asleep almost instantly. Lying on my back, his head was against mine and I could feel his breath on my shoulder. In the years since I met him that was one thing I could never get over. No matter what the situation was, feeing his breath on any part of me always brought me back to the first time he brought me to his house.

~

I couldn't fall asleep. Whether it was the dull ache in my body or of my mind, I had grown accustomed to both. It was hard for me to imagine life any other way. I would never survive without Henley. I needed him and for him to need me in return, was more than I could have ever hoped for.

Every time I closed my eyes, I could see my father's face and almost hear him saying the same things to me as Henley said. Guilt filled me as I wished I could go back and tell my father I was sorry. There wasn't a moment growing up that I didn't make things more difficult for him and most of the time it was intentional.

Recalling the day my mother sat on the side of my bed, trying to defend my father's actions to me. She asked me what I would do if I had thought my life would turn out one way and it didn't. At the time, I was so mad at her and my father, I didn't actually listen to what she was saying. The more I thought about it, the more I realized, I still didn't know the answer to that question. I didn't have a plan for my life. I never planned for my future or thought of what would happen to me when I grew up. Maybe that was my problem. With no goals or aspirations, what did I have to lose by not following rules or giving into authority.

Finally feeling myself drift off, I decided, this is where I belonged. Henley was my life.

~L~w~H~

It took a few months before I healed enough, outside and inside, to have lunch with Emerson. He was sitting at a table in a local restaurant. Trying to prepare myself for the way he looked at me, I took slow controlled breaths. Emerson never asked questions or gave advice, he just assured me that he was there and always would be.

Sliding into the seat across from him, I watched his thoughtful eyes look me over.

"I am glad you came," he assured in a soft voice.

Nodding, I said, "I am too."

Looking down as the waiter brought our food to the table, he shared, "I ordered for you."

Since I had missed several lunches with him, I questioned, "What if I hadn't shown up?"

With a light sigh Emerson replied, "I always do, whether you show up or not."

Feeling my jaw clench as my eyes involuntarily filled with tears, I breathed, "Why?"

"Because, I love you," he answered.

Shaking my head as tears rolled down my cheeks, I couldn't remember the last time I heard those words. Emerson was the first and only person who had ever said

211

them to me. I wanted to say it back but just the thought was excruciating enough.

"So how are things? Anything new?" I asked, wiping my eyes and trying to distract myself.

Emerson's eyes were sincere as he replied, "Nothing has changed, we are all the same as we were before," and I got the feeling there was more meaning behind his words than simply answering my question.

"Before what?" I questioned.

Almost at a whisper he answered, "Before you left." Feeling myself frown, I nodded.

Guilt swelled in my heart as I realized what I had done to him. Emerson was sweet, loving and kind. I had no business becoming friends with him in the first place. He couldn't help himself but I could. Quietly eating my lunch, I decided this was the last time I would meet with him.

~

When we said our goodbyes, I hugged him, allowing myself to indulge in the feeling one last time. There was a time when it was the best feeling I knew. That was before. Now, it just made me sad. I didn't want to be sad. I wanted to feel things that were within the realm of possibility. They had nothing to do with genuine emotions, they had everything to do with the ability to lose myself in a moment.

~

Shaking my head at the way Henley carefully hung clothes in the closet before counting and re-counting hangers, I sat outside his closet on the floor. Aside from my bad times, I didn't mention my father. Even then, it was mostly heaving sobs of regret.

However, my parents had been on my mind so much lately, I felt like I needed to ask, "How did you know my father?"

Immediately stopping what he was doing, Henley turned to me and asked, "Did you ask Roberts the same question at lunch?"

Confused, I said, "No, how would he know?"

Narrowing his eyes at me, he replied, "Through my uncle."

I nodded, asking, "Were ya'll friends?" as I recalled the day I witnessed Henley call my father by his first name.

Stepping out of the closet, he sat down in front of me saying, "He helped me out a few times." Then as if he missed my father, he continued, sharing, "He never treated me like.. Your father always treated me with respect. I respected him."

"Did he approve of me and you?" I questioned.

With a slight smile, he informed, "Your father talked about you all the time," before shaking his head and saying, "How disobedient you were," then added, "I couldn't stand you."

"You didn't even know me," I said.

Nodding, he shared, "I saw you once, when his friend Charles died. I was waiting at the back for him and I watched you walk off with Mason Roberts. That was the most disrespectful thing I had ever seen."

Swallowing hard, I questioned, "Why did you start asking me out then?"

His expression grew serious as he replied, "I had to."
Glancing away at first, I gave a soft smile.

"I'm not going to have lunch with Emerson anymore," I informed.

"I never told you, to stop," he said with a strange look on his face.
Scooting closer, I moved onto his lap, wrapping my arms and legs around him.

"You shouldn't have to," I admitted before pressing my lips against his.

This was where I was meant to be. We were meant to be. Henley had no one. There was only me. Since I had met Henley, there was always someone else. Parents, friends, I had other people in my life. Now, finally letting go of everything in my life but him, he was all I needed. It took almost six years for me to completely surrender myself to him. And now I had.

~L~w~H~

I grew more devoted to Henley every day. Coming to terms with the fact that I would never be able to make up for the way I was with my father, I gave my all to him. He consumed my entire life. There was not a moment in the day when Henley wasn't a thought in my mind.

~

Standing in front of the bathroom mirror, I was relieved the huge bruise on my cheek was finally gone. I still had remnants around my wrist and on my side from that afternoon a few weeks ago and some new ones on my leg and shoulder from the previous night but as long as my face was clear, I could leave the house.

Stepping out of the bathroom, I looked at Henley sitting on the bed.

"Are you going somewhere?" he asked.

Nodding, I answered, "I am going to get some donuts."

"Really?" he questioned like I was lying to him.

He was always cautious after things got out of hand.

Taking a deep breath, I nodded, saying, "Unless you want to."

Softening his expression, he reached out and grabbed my arm, pulling me onto the bed.

Rolling on top of me, he said, "I don't think I have ever seen you eat donuts before."

"Yeh, I never really liked 'em but I was dreaming about eating them. I woke up starving," I shared.

A wide smile spread across his face as he said, "I can't have you starve. I'll go get you some."

"Cream filled," I informed before he started kissing me. Wrapping my legs around his waist, I almost forgot about my donuts until my stomach started to growl.

Loud enough for us both to hear it, he pulled back, saying, "I'll be back."

Kissing him a few more times before I let him go, I was all kinds of hungry now.

~

After Henley brought me my donuts, he had to run to his shop. I still wanted more than just food when he came back but staring at the box of a dozen cream filled donuts, I was sure there was enough to occupy me until he returned.

~

When Henley returned, I had fallen asleep on the couch. Feeling kisses trailing my neck, I slowly opened my eyes and sighed.

Making his own I want you sound, he lifted me off of the couch and carried me to the bathroom. After thoroughly brushing my teeth, I was ready for him.

~

Still full from the donuts and satisfied in every other way from Henley, I laid in bed while he took a shower.

Stepping to the bed after his shower, he leaned over me.
"Did you eat the whole box?" he asked.
Shaking my head, I replied, "I threw the box away."
Cracking a smile, he said, "Was it empty?"
A little embarrassed, I actually ate twelve donuts in one sitting, I nodded, saying, "They were good."
Henley laughed a little before he kissed me and said, "Do you need anything when I come back?"
Nodding, I replied, "I'm gonna need all sorts of things when you get back."
"I won't be long," he assured.
"I'll be right here waiting," I shared before he kissed me and left to go back to his shop.

~

I fell asleep again, but woke up suddenly feeling queasy. Eating a dozen donuts was clearly not the smartest thing I had ever done. The moment I stood up, I had to run to the bathroom. I almost didn't make it. Resting my head against the side of the bathtub, I thought, 'I will never eat another donut as long as I live'.

~L~w~H~

Convinced I had food poisoning, I was sick for three days. On the fourth day, I finally stopped throwing up because I stopped eating all together. Small sips of water, was all I could tolerate. Knowing that wasn't a good thing, I called the first doctor I found in the phone book and begged to be seen. Henley was at his shop when I made the call so I drove myself when the nurse said I could be seen if I showed up right away.

~

The nurse at the front was very polite as she handed me a form to fill out. She wasn't as polite when I read the sentence 'first day of last menstrual cycle' and I threw up on her clip board. Even though I apologized several times, she gave me a dirty look when she shoved a cup at me and sent me to the bathroom.

~

Sitting on the examination table, I tried to think positive. Maybe I had the flu or was dying, anything would be better than the alternative.

~

Walking into the room, a tall middle aged woman with dark brown hair and eyes to match, closed the door behind herself.

"I am Dr. Brin, Rennillia," she greeted.

Nodding, I offered, "Just Ren," before asking, "Am I going to be alright?"

With a pleasant smile, she replied, "Yes. Everyone's body reacts a little differently to pregnancy."

"What?" I snapped at her, before blurting, "I'm not pregnant!"

Giving me a confused look she said, "Pardon me?"

Shaking my head, I insisted, "I can't be."

Giving me a compassionate smile, Dr. Brin said, "Let's get your PAP out of the way and then we will talk."

Nodding at her I thought, 'why can't I be dying?'

~

Dr. Brin's examination was almost as bad as my first time with Henley. I tried to relax but I just couldn't. When my examination was over, she stepped out so I could get dressed.

~

Rolling her chair in my direction, Dr. Brin placed her hands on her knees.

"I assume this was not a planned pregnancy," she started before questioning, "Was it forced?"

Confused at first, I quickly understood what it must have looked like with the bruising.

Shaking my head at her, I explained, "Sometimes we get carried away."

After scowling at me, she stated, "Do you have any questions?"

"Yes," I blurted before asking, "I mean we always use something, how could this have happened? Could you be wrong?"

Pursing her lips, she informed, "You are pregnant."

The seriousness in her voice caused me to panic.

Shaking my hands, I tried hard not to cry, saying, "He doesn't...I don't...I just...this can't...I...I...can't."

"Take a moment to calm down, you have options," she stated.

Taking deep breaths, it took me a minute to calm down enough to ask, "Options?"

With a short exhale, Dr. Brin informed, "There is the option of adoption. There is also...," a sharp pain in my chest caused me to cut her off, saying, "No, I mean, I didn't mean I didn't want... I don't know."

"Your next appointment is in one month. Take some time to adjust to the idea of having a baby. When you return, you may feel differently," she advised.

Nodding at her, I hopped off of the examination table.

Dr. Brin handed me a paper to take to the nurse in the front.

As I took it she stated, "One prescription is for prenatal vitamins, the other is to help with your nausea."

"Thank you," I mumbled, mostly in shock at this point.

Before I made it out of the room, Dr. Brin imparted, "Ren, sometimes life makes decisions for us that we are unable to make for ourselves."

Almost in tears again, I nodded.

~

When I arrived at Henley's, he was already back, from his shop. Walking in the front door, I found him standing inside waiting for me.

"Where were you?" he snapped.

Swallowing hard, I said, "I still wasn't feeling good so I went to the doctor."

Narrowing his eyes at me he questioned, "What doctor?"

Not quite ready for this, I asked, "What?"

"What was the doctor's name?" he growled, grabbing the front of my shirt and pulling me close."

I actually had to think for a minute before answering, "Dr. Brin."

Slapping me hard, he yelled, "Don't lie to me."

My eyes instantly welled up with tears, as I breathed, "I'm not."

Grabbing my keys out of my hand before leaning so close his breath was on my mouth, he ordered, "Don't leave this house."

Nodding, I watched him walk out of the front door.

~

Lying in the bathtub I tried to stop crying. What the hell was I going to do? This couldn't be happening. She had to be wrong. How could the doctor be certain I was pregnant? Every time I thought of the word pregnant, I started to hyperventilate. Finally, I decided, I wasn't going to think about it anymore. When Henley came home, I would think about it again. Maybe if I took a nap, I would wake up and this wouldn't be happening at all.

~

After Henley returned, I decided to start off small. If he thought having a kid was worse than a pet, then I needed to find a way to ease him into the news. Starting with the idea of getting a puppy might be a good start. I had a month to see how things went.

Standing in front of him as he sat on the couch, I took a few deep breaths.

"I need to talk to you," I started.

Without looking at me, he snapped, "Are you going to tell me where you really were?"

I gave a heavy sigh before saying, "I was at the doctor's office."

Glaring up at me, he stated, "What?"

With a deep breath I said, "I want a puppy."

When he only stared I me, I thought 'ok, this might not be so bad.'

"I will take really good care of it and make sure it doesn't make a mess."

Standing up right in front of me, he assured, "If you bring anything into my house, I will get rid of it."

Suddenly defensive, I shouted, "How can you say that?"

Grabbing the front of my shirt, he growled, "Nothing comes in my house. NOTHING!"

Tears filled my eye and before I could say anything else, he pushed me backwards.

Falling over the coffee table, the moment I hit the floor, I thought, 'what if?' In that moment I knew, the fear I felt for someone I didn't know, a stranger, was all I cared about.

~

Lying on the living room floor, crying, I couldn't make myself get up until Henley stepped back in. Pulling me up by my arm, I quickly got to my feet and jerked away.

Pulling me against him, he whispered, "Come to bed." Nodding, I followed him to the room.

My mind was racing. All sorts of things that never occurred to me caused fear and panic when his hand slid under my shirt.

Grabbing his hand through my shirt, I said, "Stop." Moving his hands down to my hips, he tugged me closer.

"Stop it," I gripped.

Sliding on top of me, he kissed me. As my body seemed to react on its own, my mind flashed with visions of every fight Henley and I ever had.

Turning my head to the side, I stressed, "No."

Pulling back slightly with a vile expression, he questioned, "Because of a disgusting animal?"

Somewhere in my mind I knew he was still talking about a puppy but at the same time, if he thought children were worse than pets and pets were disgusting…

Staring right into his eyes, I stated, "Don't touch me." Pushing off from my shoulders, he rolled off of me.

~

Unable to concentrate on just one thing, what was I going to do? I couldn't leave, I needed him. I couldn't stay because my little stranger needed me. Not being able to sleep, the only consistent thing that ran through my mind was, this can't be real.

~L~w~H~

Sitting on the floor in the closet, I wrapped my arms around my legs, resting my head on my knees. After making my decision, I made it as far as the closet. Glaring at my black duffle, I tried to think. Clenching my teeth every time I started to reach out and touch it, I felt like I was having a heart attack.

Closing my eyes, I counted to ten before grabbing hold of my duffle. Pulling it to me, I slowly unzipped it. Trying not to hyperventilate, I looked at the contents inside. I thought for sure the shoes I used to stomp mud all over the floor were gone. They sat, perfectly clean, right on top of my clothes. Standing up, I drug my bag out of the closet.

Taking my shoes out of my bag, I set them on the floor next to the bed. I grabbed a t-shirt, jeans, a bra and my panties that had set in my bag in the corner of Henley's closet for a little over six years and placed them on the bed.

After changing out of the clothes I had on and neatly folding them before carefully placing them back into the drawer, I put my old clothes on. Slipping my shoes on, I was leaving with only what I had when I turned up on his doorstep, except for my reason.

I knew it was morning without having to look at the clock. Lying on the mattress, I took out of Sophia's room, I wasn't sure if I wanted to get up. My whole body hurt, but the ache in my chest was the worst. Whether it was from lack of sleep, crying or the weight of everything going on, I didn't want to move.

While my mind ticked away with everything I needed to do, my body remained still. I felt responsible for everything, and at the same time, in control of nothing. Then, an unexpected wave of pride rolled through me, and I sat up.

Chapter 1

I splashed cold water on my face, wishing I hadn't cried all night. It was early enough to take my time getting ready, to meet with Salvador before I picked up Sophia. No matter what I did, my eyes stayed red and puffy. I wasn't looking forward to going downstairs, and having Jackson see me like this either. Giving up, I did my best to put on a pleasant face as I headed downstairs.

In an effort to not be starving later, even though I wasn't particularly hungry, I fixed myself a piece of toast. Seated at the kitchen table, I kept my eyes on my plate when Jackson walked in. After pouring himself a bowl of cereal, he sat down at the table with me.

There was a hint of pity in his voice when he asked, "How are you this morning?"

I nodded and continued to eat my toast.

"When are we heading to your meeting?"

Keeping my eyes down, I replied, "We're not. I'm calling a driver."

It took him a minute before he asked, "Do you want me to get Sophia for you?"

"No, I'm picking her up after."

"Is there anything I can do for you?" he questioned, almost pleading.

I looked up at him. "Yea, you can be normal."

The second he saw my eyes, I could feel his heart going out to me.

Before he said something that made me want to cry, I urged, "Please don't Jacks. I'm fine."

"You don't look fine."

"I know. I am though. I'm just... I'm sad, but I'll be okay."

I quietly finished my toast while he ate his cereal.

When I was ready, the driver arrived, and I was on my way. Careful not to be found out, I asked the driver to stop at a diner on the way to get Sophia.

As the driver parked the car, I informed, "I am going to get a cup of coffee. I will be right back."

The driver replied, "Yes ma'am."

Opening the door for myself, I took a deep breath, and stepped out of the car.

At the counter, I ordered a large black coffee to-go then stepped to the side. Glancing at the back corner, I saw Salvador, seated alone at a table.

He appeared pleased as I walked to his table. "This is a pleasant surprise."

"I haven't made a decision yet."

With a sly grin, he narrowed his eyes at me.

"Is it possible you simply wished to see me again?"

"It occurred to me, I'm unable to make a decision without knowing what you want from me."

Another slight smile preceded, Salvador complimenting, "I'm pleased you asked. I have to admit, I would have thought less of you, had you agreed without knowing what I require."

"Well?" I questioned, not being fond of his compliments.

With a slow blink, he replied "I'm not sure. However, I know that it's you I need."

Struck by momentary brilliance, I offered, "Then I propose we both take a month to consider...things. Then, meet again."

Salvador gave me a slow nod of agreement before assuring, "I look forward to our next meeting."

My number was called and with a sarcastic grin, I excused myself from his presence.

I took my coffee from the counter, walked out of the dinner, and slid into the car. It was possible that being hurt and disappointed from the night before made this meeting with Salvador easier than the first. However, the fact that I had a whole month to think and plan also gave me a settled feeling.

When arrived at Mrs. Thomas', she opened the door before I knocked.

"Sophia just fell asleep."

"Oh, it's kind of early for her nap."

"She was very upset when Jacks left to go home last night. It was so sad. She was up pretty late."

"Aww, you should have called me, I would have gotten her."

She gave me an odd look. "It was your anniversary."

"It wouldn't have mattered." I assured with a pang of sadness.

Taking a closer look at me, Mrs. Thomas asked, "Have you been crying? What happened?"

Shaking my head, I sighed, "It's just... He doesn't..."

"Let's go sit down." She suggested, patting me on the shoulder.

I followed her to the den, and sat down on the couch with her.

I knew I couldn't tell her everything, but at the moment, I was in serious need of a mother daughter talk. Since I had no mother, and she had no daughter, I hoped cashing in her, 'If you ever need to talk,' offer was as welcome as I needed it to be.

"Hert wants me and loves me, but not in the right way."

"There's a wrong way?"

"He wants me...when he wants me. Which I guess is fine. But he doesn't have room in his life for me other than that."

"I see. He wants you, not the relationship."

"Yea. I guess, I'm really not that surprised, but it hurts...because I thought he did."

Teary eyed, all the feelings from the night before spilled out.

"Plus, it's insulting for him to think I would be okay with an arrangement, that I'm just some..."

"I don't know him very well. You say he loves you, but honey, no one who really loves you makes you feel like that."

No matter how upset I was, I couldn't help defending Hert.

"He's had a really hard life. Maybe he just doesn't know how, ya know."

Mrs. Thomas gave me a blank stare, at first.

"Well who hasn't? I was eight when my parents died, and even though it put a terrible financial burden on my aunt and uncle, they took me in anyway. JP's parents all but disowned him when he married me, and I planned on having six children and couldn't. But, you know what, through everything neither JP nor my family ever made me feel unloved."

"We aren't like you and Mr. Thomas. Our families weren't that great when we had them."

"JP and I's marriage hasn't always been easy, but we never lost sight of each other, because above all else, we were committed to each other. You and Hert are married and that is serious. I don't think anyone should take their vows lightly or not try to make it work. Honestly honey, when someone really loves you, they never make you question if you deserve it or if they do... Because it's a gift," she imparted with a soft smile.

I burst into tears.

We sat there on the couch for a while. I cried as she consoled. When Sophia woke up Mrs. Thomas suggested I take a little nap, and calm down so I didn't upset her. With a slight headache, I agreed and curled up on the couch.

The sound Sophia giggling and Jackson's voice woke me. Sitting up, I used the tissues Mrs. Thomas left for me, and tried to look like I hadn't just cried my eyes out.

Obviously checking on me, Mrs. Thomas walked in, asking, "Feeling better?"

"Can Sophia and I stay tonight?"

"I would like that," she replied with a smile.

When Jackson walked in with Sophia, she instantly threw her arms out to me.

As he set her down with me, I hugged and kissed her forehead, saying, "I love you."

I held her as she snuggled up with me on the couch.

"You wanna stay for dinner, and then head back to the house?" Jackson asked.

Before I could answer, Mrs. Thomas informed, "Ren is staying here tonight."

Jackson gave me a confused look as I nodded at him.

"I'm going to start dinner," Mrs. Thomas shared, before leaving the room.

He sat down on the floor in front of me, questioning, "Did something happen?"

Confused at first, I realized that Jackson expected me to pick Sophia up, and head back to the house after meeting with Salvador.

"No, it went fine. I got over here and kinda fell apart on your mom."

"I was worried about you," he admitted.

"I'm sorry."

"You're lucky this was the first place I checked and you were here. I was fixing to go around shakin' people down for information," he assured with a smile.

I laughed a little, asking, "Are you gonna stay here too?"

"I would but I'm pretty sure my mom won't like that idea."

"Yea, but you're staying for dinner right?"

With a wink he offered, "I'll stay until they tell me to go home."

Smiling at him, I nodded.

After dinner, Mr. Thomas sat at the table with stacks of folders and a laptop. While Mrs. Thomas and I played with Sophia, I noticed Jackson sit down at the table with his dad.

Smiling, Jackson asked him, "Need an extra pair of eyes?"

Mr. Thomas laughed out loud, teasing, "Boy with those glasses you'd think you could see through the paper."

Mrs. Thomas overheard them too and fussed, "Stop picking on him, JP."

Smiling at them, I shook my head mumbling to myself, "I like his glasses."

I stood up and took Sophia with me to Jackson's old room. I changed her and rocked her to sleep before returning to the den.

"Sorry I don't have a bed for you, I made up the couch," Mrs. Thomas shared.

Chiming in from the kitchen, Jackson commented, "You could always curl up in the crib with Sophia in my old room."

Sticking my tongue out at him, I assured, "The couch is fine."

Mrs. Thomas walked up behind Mr. Thomas, patting him on the shoulder as she asked, "Are you about done? It's getting late."

Shaking his head and rubbing his forehead, Mr. Thomas answered, "We're behind and until we're not shorthanded anymore…"

Jackson looked at his parents, and offered, "I'll do it."

"Jacks you're on vacation," Mrs. Thomas reminded.

Jackson laughed, assuring, "I don't mind. Besides dad's old, he needs his rest."

Hopping up, Mr. Thomas replied, "Oh yea, bet I can still take you."

Mrs. Thomas rolled her eyes, saying, "Okay, boys," as Mr. Thomas tried to put Jackson in a head lock.

Laughing at them, I told the Thomas' goodnight as I went to the den, and Mr. and Mrs. Thomas went to their room.

It didn't take long for me to realize my nap earlier in the day was making it hard for me to fall asleep. It was either that, or the fact that there was still a piece of pear cake in the kitchen left over from dinner. Mrs. Thomas' pear cake was the most delicious desert in the world.

I decided it was the pear cake and walked to the kitchen.

Smiling at Jackson, as I passed him, I shared, "That was really nice of you."

Without breaking his concentration, Jacks nodded.

Thinking the cake could wait a minute, I sat at the table with him and asked, "You want some help?"

Jackson looked up from the papers and questioned, "You wanna help?"

"If I can."

Jackson smiled at me before he handed me a stack of folders, and instructed, "Highlight every third line then put them in order by date."

With the two of us working together, we finished in a little under an hour.

When the work was done, I hopped up from the table.

"Are you fixing to go home?"

"Yea, it's pretty late. Are you going to bed?"

"I might watch some TV in the den. I'm not really tired now."

"I'll hang out and watch a movie with you if you want," he offered.

"Aren't you supposed to go home? I don't want you to get in trouble." I teased.

Jackson laughed, "I'm a grown man."

Shaking my head at him, I walked to the den and sat down on the couch.

He put a movie on then walked to the kitchen, and came back with the piece of cake I had forgotten about, until it was in his hand.

"Ah, that was mine," I complained as he took a bite.

Giving me a strange look, he sat down on the couch saying, "I didn't see your name on it."

"Your mom made it because it's my favorite, so the last piece should be mine."

"It's my favorite too," he disagreed.

In a hushes tone, as not to wake his parents, I fussed, "Give me the cake,"

Refusing, he laughed, "No."

Crossing my arms, I sat there pouting.

"Okay, pouty baby, we'll share it."

I held out my hand and he shook his head saying, "I'll hold it, I don't trust you."

Giving him a stupid look, I leaned over to take a bite. When Jackson moved the cake up to my mouth, I quickly grabbed hold of his hand and shoved the rest into my mouth.

"I can't believe you just did that," he laughed as he ate the tiny bits of smushed cake from his fingers.

Unable to reply with my mouth full, I nodded, and smiled with my cheeks filled with Mrs. Thomas' delicious pear cake.

It took me a little bit, but I finally swallowed my huge bite of cake. Feeling incredibly proud of myself for high jacking the last bit, I looked over at him.

"Told ya the last piece was mine."

"I guess, I should be grateful I didn't lose a finger."

Rolling my eyes, I scoffed, "Oh, whatever."

Scooting right next to me, he shoved his thumb in my face.

"Yes huh, you bit me, see."

Turning to face him, I argued, "No, I didn't. Let me see."

I pulled his hand down, and inspected his thumb.

Pointing to a tiny red mark on his thumb, he insisted, "Right there."

"Okay, ya big baby," I admitted, and kissed his thumb.

When I leaned back up his face was turning red, and he was starting to fidget.

The moment quickly turned serious as I realized how close we were. Still holding his hand I rubbed my thumb against the tiny red mark I just kissed. Jackson appeared as though he wanted to say something, but couldn't. Oddly enough, I seemed to be having the same problem. When we heard Mrs. Thomas clear her throat from the doorway, Jackson instantly jumped up.

Pointing at me, Jackson fussed, "She bit me!"

Outraged, I pointed back, saying, "He tried to eat my piece of pear cake."

Mrs. Thomas looked at us like we were ridiculous before patting Jackson on the back, and scolding, "Now this really should go without saying, but Ren is our guest, and you should share." She then turned to me and said, "And no biting."

In unison, Jackson and I replied, "Yes, Ma'am."

Shaking her head at both of us, she said, "Night kids."

I waited to hear her door shut after she left the room.

"Tattle tale."

"You did bite me," he stated.

Giving him a stupid look, I blurted, "So you told your mommy on me?"

"Did you want me to tell her she was interrupting us?"

The knot returned to my stomach as I questioned, "Was she?"

Jackson stared at me for a moment, then shook his head.

"No...I'm gonna go."

Conflicted, I nodded back at him as he got up and left.

After turning the TV off, I sighed and walked back to the couch. With an 'ugh' thought, I laid down. It was good that when the friendship line started to slip for one of us, the other one popped it back into place. Jackson and I were spending way too much time together. We were two grown people who were friends, and cared deeply for each other. It was only natural, with everything else that was happening, for something to almost happen.

As mad as I was at Hert, I still wanted him to come back. Even though there was no way in hell at this point, I wanted anything to do with him; it didn't mean I instantly stopped loving him. In addition to that, having Hert back at the house would definitely limit the close calls Jackson and I were having. With another heavy sigh, I closed my eyes and decided if I spent most of the day here at the Thomas' going back to the house with Jackson tomorrow night would be fine.

Next and final book in the series

Rennillia 3- May 19, 2016

Rennillia Series

Rennillia1

There was some comfort in the realization that we were all horribly flawed.

Rennillia2

The truth is simple. It's what comes after that makes things complicated.

Rennillia:Prequel

Sometimes, you have to go back to the beginning to get to the end.

Rennillia3

There comes a time in every man's life, when he has to face the things he has done.
May 19, 2016

Marked Heart Series

Enduring Everything
MH#1
Available Now

Time doesn't always heal old wounds. Often time makes them worse. Especially when you push those wounds to the back of your mind and focus on the life you want to lead. Then the day comes when you finally have everything. It is then, you realize that nothing ever goes away.

Charlotte
MH#2
Available Now

The true measure of a person's worth lies not within what they can offer you but what you have to offer them. No matter how desirable, are they worth your time, patience, forgiveness, loyalty, friendship, love, respect, understanding, compassion, trust? If not, they are worth more than you have to offer. They deserve for you to let them go.

One Penny
MH#3
Available Now

Foolish is the heart that leaves itself open to falling in love. Reckless is the person who steps away from tradition to claim a life of their own. Irreplaceable is the moment one takes the risk.

C&A Novella
MH#3.5
Available Now
He was all the things she really wanted and never bothered to look for in a man. He was also the most stubborn jackass she had ever met.

She was an infuriating pain in the ass, and he'd be damned straight to hell if he had to spend even one day without her by his side.

Marked Heart
MH#4
New Release
A marked heart, longing for the one is nothing more than a restless heart, burdened by a lie.

Marked Heart Series
Complete Box Set
Four full-length stand alone novels and one novella interconnecting four couples that will make you fall in love, laugh, cry, swoon, and believe in second chances.

#FREE C&A Serial

If you enjoyed The Marked Heart novels, then this is my gift to you. Starting November 20, 2015 on my website there will be a free C&A monthly web serial. Although Charlotte and Auggie are the focus of the serial, many of the MH characters will make appearances.

www.BrokenBirdMedia.com

Acknowledgments

I've gone back and forth, several times, on what to write in this section. Technically, this could be considered a dedication, but I feel it fits in the acknowledgements. So, here it goes...

I would like to acknowledge those that fell and were able to pick themselves back up.

The ones who, at one time, thought there was no end in sight, and found a reason to keep going.

Those brave souls that conquered their fears, doubts, and demons.

Even though they were afraid of the outcome, they saw beyond the present, and took a step toward a better future.

Every person who has sifted through the pain, broken pieces, and regrets in life and decided it wasn't over.

To all the Broken Birds out there, I acknowledge you for being the beautiful badass that you are.

If you or someone you know is experiencing abuse call the National Domestic Violence Hotline at 1–800–799–SAFE (7233)

About the Author

M. Sembera was born in Baton Rouge, Louisiana and now lives in Brazoria, Texas with her husband, three kids, three dogs and two cats. After writing her first short story when she was in high school, M. instantly fell in love with writing. However, life sometimes gets in the way of aspirations and it wasn't until years later, when her life calmed down, M. was able to start writing again.

'For me, each new book I write or character I create feels like the first time and I find myself falling in love with writing all over again'

Receive updates and info on author M. Sembera's New Releases, WIPs, Sales and Giveaways by subscribing to M's monthly newsletter: http://eepurl.com/bdJ_Uj

Work in Progress

Untitled WIP ©M. Sembera

Everyone has their own side to a story. This is mine. ~Abigail

Excerpt:

The days seemed to grow shorter as I looked forward to spending them with Soman. Nothing changed between us aside from one time when he touched my cheek to retrieve a fallen eyelash from it. He wished for us to always be together and I kissed his cheek in return. Neither of us said anything about our moment once it was over. Ours was a friendship like no other. It felt as though destiny brought us together. That was until fate had other plans.